Faith, Hope & Love

by

Kimberly Rae Jordan

Other titles available

~*~ Kimberly Rae Jordan ~*~
(Christian Romances)

Marrying Kate
Amazon Kindle ASIN: B00BORR1PK

Faith, Hope & Love
Amazon Kindle ASIN: B00B9DN8OM

Waiting for Rachel (*Those Karlsson Boys: Book 1*)
Amazon Kindle ASIN: B00C8X8Q5S

Worth the Wait (*Those Karlsson Boys: Book 2*)
Amazon Kindle ASIN: B00ECZ6QT8

A Little Bit of Love:
A Collection of Christmas Romance Short Stories
Amazon Kindle ASIN: B00EEUN48W

~*~ K.R. Jordan ~*~
(Sweet Romances)

Act of Love (*Typecast Christmas Collection*)
Amazon Kindle ASIN: B00FDKBUZQ

DEDICATION

To my husband who has encouraged me to pursue my dreams and has taken the time to read my stories. After not writing for many years, his support has allowed me to once again step into a world I love as I create the stories of my heart to share with you.

To Susette for the never ending encouragement to get my books out there for readers to enjoy. Your persistence has paid off! Thank you for not giving up on me and for so generously sharing your experiences and knowledge of this ePublishing industry.

Be still, and know that I am God;
I will be exalted among the nations,
I will be exalted in the earth!

Psalm 46:10

Prologue

A rooster crowed in the distance, coaxing Cassie from a deep sleep. She pulled her pillow over her head to block out the noises coming from beyond the screen window. It didn't work. Groaning, Cassie turned over and opened her eyes. Sunlight streamed into the room. Though the brightness blinded her temporarily, she was glad for the sunshine. As the wife of a pilot, she'd always be happier to see the sun than clouds.

As she sat up and stretched, Cassie realized the last thing she remembered from the night before had been reading a book. Leaning over the side of the bed, she spotted it lying face down on the floor. Cassie grinned. She knew tiredness was one of the symptoms, but she hadn't realized exactly how tired she'd be.

Resting back against the headboard, Cassie laid a hand on her still flat stomach. She planned to tell Quinn about it that night. The pregnancy test she'd taken the day before only confirmed what she'd suspected for the past week. Quinn had apparently been too busy to notice that her usual clockwork cycle was off.

Cassie knew he was going to be excited. They'd decided to start trying for a family after they had settled into their new home on the missionary center in Colombia. Cassie had begun to wonder if something was wrong when, after three months, she still hadn't gotten pregnant but the fourth month had obviously been the one.

Cassie heard the water shut off in the bathroom and knew Quinn had finished his shower. She slid out from under the sheet and stood next to the bed working the kinks out of her neck. She was so thankful that as of yet she'd had no problems with morning sickness. Cassie hoped it stayed that way for the entire pregnancy.

As a nurse-midwife she'd helped plenty of women go through their pregnancies and deliveries but this was all new to her as a personal experience. She grinned at the thought of being the pregnant one for a change.

Thoughts of her plan to tell Quinn filled Cassie's mind as she went into the bathroom. Quinn, clad in a pair of jeans, stood in front of the mirror shaving.

"Morning, Sunshine." Quinn smiled and leaned down to give her a kiss. He took the towel from around his neck and wiped the smudge of shaving cream he'd left on Cassie's cheek before cleaning off his own face.

Cassie slid her arms around his bare waist and kissed him again. He smelled of soap, toothpaste, and shaving cream. As much as she loved the cologne Quinn usually wore, Cassie also loved the scent of him fresh from the shower.

"You must have been pretty tired last night," Quinn commented, running a hand up and down her back. "I looked over and there you were, sound asleep. Snoring."

"I do not snore." Cassie pulled back to give him a look of playful disgust. "You're the one who snores."

Quinn chuckled "Betcha couldn't prove that about last night. You were out cold."

Cassie gave Quinn another kiss before moving out of his embrace. "Yeah, I was pretty tired. I feel great this morning though."

"Good. I'd hate to think you're coming down with something."

Cassie almost laughed. Oh yes, she was coming down with something. Nine months of something.

"You're going to be back in time for supper, right?" Cassie asked.

"Yep." Quinn shrugged into the shirt that had been hanging on the back of the bathroom door. "I have two flights today but as long as the weather holds, there should be no delays. Of course the first flight may take a while, depending on how long it takes the guys coming with me to do what they need to."

"Oh right. They're going to try and set up a generator and a computer, right?"

Quinn nodded. "Hopefully everything goes smoothly."

"I'll pray it does." Cassie followed Quinn out of the bathroom. "So, what do you want for breakfast?"

"Nothing fancy. Some toast and fruit would be fine."

Cassie headed for the small kitchen and began to prepare their breakfast. By the time Quinn joined her everything was ready.

They held hands and Quinn said grace. "Father, we commit our day to you. May Your will be done and Your name glorified in all that we do. Be with Cassie here at home, and with me and the guys during our flight. Give us good weather and safety. Be with our family back in Minneapolis and keep them healthy and safe. Thank you for this food and for Cassie for preparing it for us. In Jesus' name, amen."

"Amen," Cassie echoed.

They talked about their day as they ate and then had a short devotional together. When the time came for Quinn to leave for work, Cassie walked him to the front door.

Bright sunlight and warmth embraced them as they stepped out onto the front porch of their small home. Cassie loved the missionary center where they lived. Green grass and huge leafy trees abounded on the center, giving it a lush, vibrant appearance. She imagined their child running barefoot along packed dirt paths and freshly cut grass. What a wonderful place for a child to grow up.

"Have a good day, Sunshine," Quinn said, leaning down to kiss her.

Cassie held him tight and returned his kiss. "Fly with God, Quinn. I'll see you later. I'm planning a special dinner for tonight so don't be late."

"I'll try not to be." Quinn rubbed his nose to hers. "Love you."

"Love you too." Cassie captured his face between her hands and gave him one last kiss.

Quinn headed off toward the nearby airplane hanger with a smile on his face. A smile lingered on Cassie's lips too as she went back inside to clean up the dishes from breakfast.

Forty-five minutes later she heard the airplane engine roar to life. She was familiar with the different sounds and knew from the acceleration of the engine that the plane was taxiing out onto the runway. Wiping her hands on a dishtowel, Cassie stepped out the back door.

She could see the sunlight glinting off the white and blue metal of the small Cessna Quinn piloted. Cassie raised a hand to shade her eyes and watched the plane taxi to the end of the runway and turn around. It sat for a minute before beginning a gradually increasing pace down the runway.

Cassie waved as the plane went by. She didn't know if Quinn saw her, but she liked to think the small tip of the wing as the plane soared into the clear, blue sky was Quinn's way of saying good-bye to her.

She stood watching the plane grow smaller and smaller, a hand splayed against her stomach. "There goes your daddy, little one. He's going to be the best daddy in the whole world. I love him very much and can't wait to tell him about you tonight."

After the plane had disappeared from sight, Cassie returned to the kitchen and her preparations for their special dinner.

Four hours later a knock interrupted her as she sat at the computer writing emails to family back in Minneapolis. Cassie went to answer the door thinking one of the pregnant women living on the missionary center had stopped by to visit and have a quick check-up.

When she saw Aaron Johnson, the center administrator, and his wife Cecily standing on the other side of the screen door her heart skipped a beat. They didn't usually make casual visits in the middle of a workday, and even through the screen Cassie could see the seriousness of their expressions.

Something was wrong.

Cassie stood frozen several feet from the door. As long as she didn't open the door. As long as they didn't tell her. Everything would be okay.

"Hi Cassie. Can we come in?" Aaron asked.

Cassie closed her eyes and pressed her hands to her stomach. Surely God wouldn't let anything happen to Quinn, not when the baby they'd prayed so hard for was finally on its way.

Chapter One

Cassie pressed down on the top of the suitcase with her knee then jerked the zipper around the corner, pulling it to meet the other one. She still had one suitcase left to pack but since it was mainly their clothing it would wait until closer to their departure date. With a grunt she hefted the bulging suitcase off the bed to the carpeted floor.

"Are you sure you're doing the right thing?"

Cassie glanced to where her sister-in-law sat perched on the window seat, her cheek resting on her drawn up knees. Even from across the room Cassie could read the concern on Renee's face. "I thought you were okay with this."

Renee straightened, then shrugged. "I was."

"And now you're not." Cassie went to sit beside her. "Why?"

"It seemed right when you first told me you were going to do this. I was glad you were getting on with your life. But now, with you leaving in less than a week..." Renee blinked and a tear slid down her cheek. "You and Jani are all I have left. I know Mom's still alive, but she doesn't even know who I am most days. And with Quinn gone too, I just hate to think of you so far away."

Cassie reached out to take Renee's hand. "We'll be able to send emails, and thanks to that fancy new digital camera you got us, I can send pictures of Jani all the time."

"So you saw through that gift, eh?" The corner of Renee's mouth lifted slightly. "Kind of selfish of me."

"Not at all. I've been wanting one for a while, and I'm glad I'll be able to send you pictures. Jani's going to miss her favorite aunt, so you're going to need to send some to us too."

Another quick smile curved Renee's lips but it didn't stay there for long. She looked intently at Cassie. "You're sure?"

Cassie leaned back against the edge of the window seat and pulled her own legs up, wrapping them with her arms. She gazed out at the big tree, bursting with thick leaves. "When I first came back from Colombia six years ago I was positive I'd never set foot on the mission field again. And that feeling stayed with me until last year."

"Until they told you that Quinn was most likely dead. That all reports they were hearing pointed to that conclusion."

Cassie didn't answer right away. Pain clenched her heart as it did whenever she thought of Quinn being dead. Somehow it hadn't gotten any easier. "Yes, when they told me that, I realized I had to move forward. And just like the first time I felt the call to be a missionary, it took a missionary speaker to open my eyes again.

"Before Quinn and I got married, we both experienced a longing to serve the Lord on the mission field. That was a longing given to each of us individually, not as a couple. It became our desire as a couple once we married but still, the Lord had called us as individuals. Now I no longer have Quinn at my side but the calling is still there. I think Quinn would have wanted me to go."

"But what if something happens to you? Or to Jani?" Cassie heard the edge of panic in Renee's voice.

Cassie knew better than to tell her that nothing would happen. After all, something had happened. Her husband, Renee's brother, had been taken hostage six years ago and was now presumed dead. The worst could, and had, happened.

"We have to trust the Lord, Renee. The mission is sending us to a place that has not had a lot of political strife. We'll be living with other missionaries who work at the hospital there. But if something does happen, we'll deal with it. Just like we dealt with what happened to Quinn."

"I don't want you to go," Renee announced, her expression set.

Cassie sighed. "I know. But right now I feel like the Lord is asking me to be willing to go. And I am."

"But how do you really know it's His will? After all, you haven't been able to rent your house nor has the doctor's office been able to find someone to replace you."

Cassie drew her brows together in a frown. Renee was right. She had been praying for both those things to happen before she left and yet neither had. But in spite of that, she still felt the Lord wanted them to prepare to leave the following week.

She glanced around the room. All but the basics, the bed and dresser, had been put into storage at Renee's. She was also leaving some furniture in the other rooms in case someone wanted to rent a furnished house. It wasn't a big deal since the house, which had been left to her by her parents, had been paid off. She wasn't worried about mortgage payments but did want someone in the house while they were gone.

"Maybe you're really not supposed to go since those two things are still up in the air."

Cassie looked at Renee, wishing she could get her sister-in-law to understand all that was in her heart. How do you explain to someone that incredible yearning, that intense desire that could only have been placed there by God? Cassie rubbed a hand over her chest. She believed with all her heart she was doing the right thing. There was no doubt in her mind the Lord had called her to take this step.

Cassie reached out and took both Renee's hands in her own and squeezed them. She looked into eyes so like Quinn's and saw the grief there. Renee would never stand in the way of God's will but right now the pain was forcing her to do things she never would have otherwise.

"I love you, Renee. You've been there for me so many times. Now I need you again. I need your support in this. I need your prayers. When Quinn and I first went to Colombia my dad and your parents were our strongest prayer allies. With our dads gone and your mom not able to understand anymore, I need you to step in and take up that challenge. To pray for us. We need you to do that. Will you?"

Tears spilled over and silent sobs wracked Renee's body. Her hands clung to Cassie's as she wept for several minutes. Finally she took a couple of deep breaths and once again met Cassie's gaze. "Yes, I will. I'm sorry for trying to turn you from the path the Lord is leading you on."

Cassie reached out and pulled Renee into a tight embrace. "No need to apologize. I know you said what you did because you're scared… so am I."

Renee straightened out of the embrace, wiping her hands across her cheeks. "You better email me all the time and send me lots of pictures. And we're gonna Skype as often as we can. If you don't I might just have to get on a plane and come see you."

Cassie grinned. "Well, if that's all it will take to get you to visit us—"

They shared laughter then, reinforcing the strong bond between them.

*****

The next morning Cassie glanced at the calendar on the wall as she stirred the pancake batter. *Six years.* In two weeks it would be six years since Quinn's kidnapping. Even though most had given up hope of him ever coming home, a tiny part of Cassie's heart continued to hold out hope that all the eyewitness reports had been wrong. That somehow they had lied or that Quinn had only been injured by the bullets and not killed.

She had not told anyone in the past year, not even Renee, that she believed Quinn was still alive. Cassie didn't know why the Lord was prompting her to the mission field again while things were still not resolved with Quinn, but she was going, trusting that when Quinn was freed, he'd join her so they could once again serve the Lord together.

Setting the bowl down, Cassie flicked on the small television sitting on the counter. She bent and retrieved the electric griddle from a low cupboard and plugged it in. While waiting for the pan to heat, Cassie listened to the newscaster begin her run-through of the day's top stories.

Once the griddle had heated, she picked up the bowl of batter and began to drizzle a scoopful onto its hot surface. The phone rang as she finished the first pancake. She set the ladle on the counter and reached for the phone. The long cord allowed her to tuck the receiver between her shoulder and ear and still pour the pancake batter.

"Hello?"

"Cassie?"

She paused. Batter dripped from the lip of the ladle to the hot surface of the griddle. A flash of hope filled her but she worked to squelch it. Disappointment had come too many times in the past.

"Aaron!" Cassie resumed pouring the batter. "How are you doing?"

"I'm fine, Cassie, just fine."

Something in Aaron's voice caught her attention. She let go of the ladle and turned from the counter, the bowl still tucked into the curve of her arm. Her heart pounded and her throat tightened. Was this good news or bad?

She swallowed. "What's up? You don't usually call this early. And it's even earlier there in California."

"We've got news."

Cassie gripped the receiver with her free hand and pressed it closer to her ear. "Good news, Aaron? Please tell me it's good news."

"It's great news, Cassie. Quinn's been released! He'll be on his way home in a few hours."

Cassie's arms went limp. The bowl slipped and hit the floor. Batter splattered her legs, the cupboards and the linoleum, but she didn't care. Aaron continued to talk though the blood had rushed to her head and her ears were ringing so she couldn't hear a word he said. Cassie sank to the floor when her legs would no longer hold her.

Quinn was alive! And coming home!

Cassie began to shake. She wrapped her arm around her knees and pulled herself into a tight ball trying to control it, but still her body trembled.

"Oh God, thank you! Thank you so much!" Tears of relief slid down her cheeks. The day she'd hoped for had finally arrived. Her family was going to be complete again. Cassie tried to suppress the sobs but relief and joy pushed them to the surface. She knew Aaron would wait until she had herself under control. He and Cecily had been with her through every high and low during the past six years.

"Mommy?"

Cassie turned and felt her heart clench anew. The petite girl standing in the doorway clad in a Barbie nightgown was finally going to get to meet her daddy.

"Oh Jani!" Cassie put the receiver down on the floor and opened her arms to her daughter. Jani moved slowly across the batter-splattered floor and stepped into her mother's arms. Cassie looked through a mist of tears at that darling face with eyes so like her father's. "Daddy's coming home."

"My daddy's coming home?" When Cassie nodded, Jani jerked out of her embrace and began to dance around the kitchen until she slipped on a patch of batter and landed on her behind on the floor. Instead of crying though, she looked up at Cassie and laughed. "My daddy's coming home!"

Cassie picked up the receiver and heard Aaron's chuckle.

"She's excited," Cassie told him.

"I can hear that. I'm so glad for the two of you."

"When can we see him, Aaron? Where is he arriving?"

Aaron chuckled. "Guess you missed that earlier,"

"I'm sorry, I was so caught up in the news about Quinn."

"No problem," Aaron told her. "It would have been simpler if the mission had been contacted first, but because of the government's involvement, they were the ones contacted. And we've suspected from the start that this was a political move. Our team is on their way down to see him and bring him home, but the government people want to talk to him as well. We're bringing him to LA and already there's a plan for a press conference. I know this isn't how you wanted it but unfortunately it's spun out of control."

"You know, Aaron, suddenly it doesn't matter. All that matters now is that he is free and on his way home. I'd fly to Siberia just so long as we're together when I get off the plane."

"And you will be," Aaron assured her.

They spent the next few minutes discussing logistics before Cassie pushed herself up off the messy floor and hung up. She turned back to find Jani still sitting on the floor, a delighted look on her small face, one that was no doubt reflected on Cassie's as well.

"We have to call Auntie," Jani exclaimed as she jumped up. "I want to tell her."

Cassie handed her the phone and watched Jani carefully punch out the number for Quinn's sister. She could hardly wait to hear Renee's reaction.

"Auntie Renee? Daddy's coming home," Jani announced proudly. She listened intently for a moment, twisting the phone cord around her small finger. Her brows drew together in a frown and she responded indignantly, "Course I'm telling the truth!"

"Here, Honey, let me talk to Auntie."

Cassie took the phone and pressed it to her ear in time to hear Renee rattle off a bunch of questions.

"He's free, and he's on his way home," Cassie told her. "I don't know anything more and frankly, that's all that matters right now."

"Of course, you're right. I just can't believe it!"

"I can't believe it either, Renee. I'm in a fog over here. My kitchen is a mess thanks to the pancake batter I dropped when I heard the news."

Renee laughed. "Want me to come over and help clean up?"

"Actually, would you mind? Not to clean up but I need your help getting stuff together. I have to fly to LA to meet him. Can Jani stay with you? I think it would be better if she didn't come to LA and get caught up in everything there." Cassie finally stopped and took a deep breath.

"I'll just phone someone to open for me at the bookstore, and I'll be right over. Don't worry, we'll have you on that plane and on your way to see Quinn in no time."

Cassie hung up the phone and leaned against the counter for a minute. Everything was going so fast. She had tons to do… starting with another shower thanks to the batter mishap. There was packing to do. Phone calls to make to get time off work.

It all whirled around her head but suddenly one frivolous, and yet alarming, thought grabbed her attention. She'd never lost those last ten pounds from her pregnancy with Jani!

A pluck on her sleeve drew her attention. She looked down at Jani and saw her pointing at the counter. Smoke was beginning to drift up from the griddle. Cassie hurried to turn the grill off and stared at the burned circles on the grill but even the prospect of burned pancakes couldn't dim the joy in her heart.

*****

Cassie reached out with her keycard, then drew her hand back, clasping it together with her other one. This was what she'd wanted, what she'd prayed for, for almost six years. She should be bursting through the door, eagerly anticipating what lay beyond. But as eager as Cassie was, a spark of fear existed deep within her. A lot had happened in six years, to both her and Quinn. Would they be able to get past the changes?

During the past few hours a lot of realities had sunk in. There were things counselors over the years had cautioned her about but until that day, Cassie had brushed aside. She'd managed to convince herself nothing could be done to Quinn that would change who he was. For some reason now she wasn't so sure. Six years was a long time. Doubts and fears buried deep within her seeped through the cracks of her confidence to the surface.

Was the man on the other side of the door her husband or a stranger?

Suddenly wishing she hadn't demanded privacy for their reunion, Cassie turned to look down the hallway of the hotel. She saw the doors of the elevator were closed and the buttons above it signaled its descent, away from her. She had to face this alone.

Aaron and Cecily had picked her up at the airport and brought her to the hotel. They'd told her Quinn had spent most the day getting checked over by medical doctors and that physically he was okay although they were still waiting for a few test results. That news had reassured her, but she got the feeling there were things they were leaving out. It was what they weren't saying that troubled her.

Cassie reached out again and this time slid the keycard in, grasped the handle and turned it.

Six years. It felt like an eternity.

The door swung open silently. Cassie stepped through the doorway into the short hall beyond. At the end of the hall lay the suite that had been provided for them. And Quinn.

Slowly Cassie shut the door and leaned back against it. She closed her eyes, praying for strength. Hearing a rustle of movement from the room at the end of the hallway, Cassie's eyes flew open and she straightened. Did he know she was there? Was he wondering why she didn't come to him?

Willing herself to put one foot in front of the other, Cassie began to walk along the plush carpet to the suite.

Bright sunlight shone through the large glass windows lining the outside wall of the suite. Silhouetted against the brightness stood a man.

"Quinn?" His name slipped past Cassie's numb lips, echoing in the silent room even though she'd barely whispered it.

The man turned toward her, and she got her first look at him. Cassie began to panic. *They've made a mistake. This isn't my Quinn.*

Even with the sun behind him obscuring most of his features she could see that this man had short—almost shaved—hair while Quinn had always worn his longer. Usually it curled at least to his collar. The man standing before her was thin and wiry, not at all like Quinn had been. No, this wasn't her Quinn.

Then the man moved from the window, freeing his features from the shadows created by the sun, and Cassie saw his eyes. They were Quinn's eyes. Not the expression in them but the color. Jani's were just like them.

With a cry, Cassie ran to him and threw her arms around him. It took a second to register that the body pressed to hers was really Quinn's. It felt unfamiliar, foreign to her. It took a little longer to realize Quinn's return embrace was slow in coming. His arms seemed to wrap around her almost reluctantly. As if he hugged her only because he knew she expected it of him.

Cassie's heart began to crack. The fear that had been slowly seeping to the surface suddenly burst through like a geyser and flooded her heart. She'd told no one about her fear, but now it seemed to be coming to life. Quinn no longer loved her. What other explanation could there be for the lack of warmth in his embrace? The lack of emotion in his welcome?

Slowly Cassie stepped back, away from the stranger. His arms fell from her back to hang limply at his sides. Cassie looked at him then, really looked. His beautiful black hair was cut so short she could see his scalp. The exposure to the sun had tanned his face a dark brown. She noticed a few more lines at the corners of his eyes and around his mouth. Dark circles lay beneath his eyes, telling more than words of his exhaustion. He was gaunt, his cheekbones starkly defined beneath tautly stretched skin.

Cassie finally looked into his eyes, afraid of what she'd see there. The color was unchanged, that deep chocolate brown, but they were expressionless. Cassie could read nothing in the eyes that had once glowed with love and affection for her.

She took a step backwards, away from the stranger who vaguely resembled her husband. As she did, her heart cried out, *this wasn't the way it was supposed to be!* The Lord had given her back her husband, but he wasn't the same man who had been taken from her six years ago.

Words didn't come to Cassie. She was at a loss to know what to say to the man standing before her. He looked at her, scrutinizing her much like she'd done him, but there was no expression on his face to let Cassie know what he thought.

"Welcome home," Cassie finally said even though they weren't in their real home yet.

Quinn glanced around the suite and then settled his gaze back on her. "Thanks."

Cassie twisted her hands together nervously. "Are you hungry? We can order something from room service if you'd like. I don't think you want to try going outside the hotel just yet. There are lots of reporters out there."

He nodded. "I know. I saw them on our way in." He ran a hand across his shorn hair. "Actually, I'm not very hungry. I'd just like a shower and bed."

Bed. Cassie's heart stuttered to a stop, then started again at an alarming speed. She'd joyfully shared her bed with Quinn before but now...

"I haven't had sleep in over twenty-four hours. I can hardly think straight." Quinn pointed to the door at the end of the living room part of the suite. "I put my stuff in that room. Your bag is in the other one."

Cassie felt relief, but disappointment shaded it. The reunion did not meet her dreams or expectations at all. It hurt that Quinn was so distant from her, but she'd been warned this might be the case. She'd chosen to ignore the warnings and now didn't know how to deal with it.

Quinn turned and disappeared through the doorway. The door shut with a soft but resounding *thud.* Cassie stared at the closed door before turning to go to her own room. She shut her door and slipped off her shoes.

For several moments she leaned against the door, her arms limp at her sides, her shoulders weighted. Five minutes. Their reunion had lasted all of five minutes. In her dreams they held each other for a good long time and then they sat down together and talked for hours about all they'd missed in each other's lives over the past six years.

Five minutes! He hadn't even asked about his family or given her the chance to tell him about Jani.

The rose-colored glasses she'd worn that the counselors over the years had tugged at to no avail had been ripped away by Quinn in five short minutes. Cassie had been so sure of Quinn's love for her and for God. She'd been so sure that nothing could significantly change the man he was. She had been wrong.

Tears threatened to spill over. Cassie didn't even bother to try and stop them. Instead, she flung herself on the bed and let grief wash over her. She curled on her side, a pillow wrapped in her arms. Cassie buried her face in it to muffle her sobs, helpless against the torrent of pain that battered her.

Chapter Two

Quinn leaned against the closed door. He knew he'd blown it with Cassie but he hadn't known how to act. He couldn't say that the reunion wasn't what he had hoped for because he'd stopped hoping for a reunion with Cassie about four years ago. It had been easier that way.

For the first couple years of his captivity in the jungle he'd dreamed of Cassie every night. He'd prayed every hour for the Lord to allow him to be reunited with her. But days had turned to weeks, weeks to months, and months to years.

The first leader of the rebels had been stern but still treated him like a human being. The next one who'd come in his second year had been more strict and more verbally abusive but still tolerable. The worst had come in year three when a monster, who had spoken English with little accent, had replaced leader number two. He had never softened towards Quinn as the others had, clearly that had been the reason he'd lasted four years as the leader.

During times of verbal abuse, Quinn could block out the Spanish words they hurled at him, but when the abuse was hurled in English he'd had no escape. And then had come the physical abuse, the beatings, and the torture by a man who seemed more American than Colombian. He'd apparently done his job because he had kept the leader position for four years. Four long years. And somewhere along the line he'd lost his faith and his dreams of Cassie.

His captors, especially in the last few years, had preyed upon emotion, so Quinn had hardened himself against it. They had continually taunted him about Cassie finding another man. They would say they'd told the world he was dead so probably his wife had found another husband.

After a while their words had the desired effect and Quinn began to wonder. Did Cassie believe him dead? Had she found another man to love? In order to protect himself in case they were telling the truth, Quinn began to distance himself from the memory of Cassie.

Now that he was free and knew the truth about the situation, Quinn didn't know how to react. He had buried his love for Cassie so deep that now that he was allowed to express it, Quinn didn't know where to find it. Or how to find it. Or if he wanted to find it.

He knew he was not the man Cassie had married. That man had died in the jungle. Would she be able to love the man who had been left in his place? Even knowing that their lives no longer traveled along the same road?

Quinn pushed away from the door and headed for the bathroom. He stopped to pick up the duffle bag he'd been given in Bogotá after being freed. It held a change of clothes and some toiletries for him. He set the bag on the floor of the bathroom and proceeded to fill the bathtub.

As he sank into the hot water Quinn groaned. His body had been tense for the past twenty-four hours. Now that he finally had a chance to relax, it actually hurt to ease the tension in his muscles.

Quinn slipped down until the water lapped at his chin, leaned his head against the back of the tub, and closed his eyes.

Cassie. Even now her scent lingered, tantalizing him, reminding him. That perfume was the one she'd worn for years. The one he'd given her for the first time on Valentine's Day, just weeks after they'd started dating. It seemed so long ago. Almost as if it had happened to another person. And in a sense, it had.

As he sat there, finally relaxed, finally free, details gradually began to filter into his mind. Memories of times when they'd been happy together. Images of Cassie as she'd been before he'd been kidnapped. Her incredible cobalt-blue eyes that sparkled like no jewel ever could. Her long blond hair, freshly washed, shining like gold in the sunlight. The feel of her in his arms.

They were images and feelings that demanded attention now that he'd seen Cassie again. He couldn't push them down inside himself anymore.

But what good would they do him? Neither of them were the same people they'd been back then. The past was the past. They were living in the present now, and there was nothing they could do to change what had happened over the past six years. The future loomed like a big black hole before Quinn. He had no idea what lay beyond that very moment.

Reluctantly Quinn left the bath as the water began to cool. He dried off, pulled on a pair of jeans and stood looking in the mirror, searching for the man he'd once been. In his mind he couldn't even picture him. It had just been one more thing he'd blocked out.

Quinn went back into the bedroom and discovered that night had fallen while he had been in the tub. He quickly snapped on all the lights in the room. He hated the darkness. In the dark even the fanciest hotel room could become the cage he'd called home for the past six years.

The bed looked inviting so Quinn climbed into it, sure he'd fall right asleep. Fifteen minutes later he realized that wasn't going to happen. The bed was too soft, the pillow too fluffy. Six years of sleeping on a straw mat with only a roll of clothing for a pillow had spoiled the pleasure of a soft bed for him.

Quinn sat up and looked at the floor. Even the carpet in the room looked too soft. His gaze went to the bathroom. The carpet in there looked more like what he'd been used to sleeping on. Soon he lay on the floor of the bathroom, a blanket over his hips, a towel beneath his head. And blessed sleep came at last.

*****

Cassie woke to darkness, swollen eyes, and a pounding headache. Slowly, she made her way through the dark bedroom to the bathroom. She didn't want to turn on the light, didn't want to see the pain and disappointment that was surely written on her face.

She stood for a few moments in the darkness before reaching out and flicking on the light switch. As she looked at herself in the harsh, unforgiving light, Cassie felt tears spring to her eyes. She blinked rapidly, determined not to give into them again. With a quick turn of her wrist she opened the faucet and bent to splash water over her aching eyes.

The torrent of emotion had passed; she had had her moment of weakness, now she needed to focus forward. Cassie had married Quinn and pledged her love to him 'till death parted them. Death hadn't won so that pledge bound her to Quinn even if the man in the room across the suite wasn't the same person she'd married. Surely something remained of the fun-loving, generous, caring man Quinn had been before the kidnapping.

Somehow Cassie had to make it work. Jani was counting on having a daddy like her other friends. And Cassie wanted her husband back. She couldn't, she wouldn't, let those rebels have the final victory by breaking up their family. They'd done that for six years. But no more. Quinn was home, and they were going to become a family again.

Cassie changed into a pair of leggings and a large T-shirt, an old one of Quinn's and, after taking an album from her bag, left the room. The suite was dark and quiet. Slowly she moved across the living room to the closed door of Quinn's room.

She started to knock but then paused. If he was sleeping she didn't want to wake him. Cassie just needed to see him, to know he was really okay, that she hadn't dreamed his return.

Light poured out as she slowly pushed open the door. Cassie froze, wondering if he was awake since all the lights appeared to be on. But still she couldn't stop herself. She'd come this far. Her heart would not be denied the opportunity to see her husband once again.

She peeked around the door. The bed was empty. Cassie quickly scanned the room but Quinn wasn't there. Fear coursed through her and propelled her further into the room. Where was he? A light came from the bathroom, so Cassie moved towards the open door. Somewhat surprised at her own boldness, Cassie paused when she first glimpsed Quinn's foot at an angle on the floor that made her think he'd fallen.

As she drew closer Cassie was able to see that Quinn did indeed lie on the floor, but not as the result of a fall like she'd feared. It looked very much like that was where he wanted to be.

Cassie stood in the doorway looking at her husband. Even in sleep he still looked tense. Quinn wore no shirt, his dark skin contrasted sharply against the light carpet of the bathroom. The ache in her heart intensified when she saw the scars on his chest. How he must have suffered over the past six years. Would he ever be able to talk about it? To put it behind him?

Sobs welled up in Cassie at the thought of Quinn in such pain. She dipped her head and cupped a hand over her mouth to keep from making a sound and disturbing Quinn. When she finally regained control, Cassie looked back up, and met a hard gaze.

Startled, Cassie gasped and stumbled back against the door. "I'm sorry." The words came out as a ragged whisper. "I just wanted to make sure you were okay. I didn't mean to wake you."

Quinn didn't say anything for a long moment, just leaned on one elbow looking at her. "I'm a light sleeper," he finally said. "I'm fine. The bed was too soft."

"Hotels aren't always known for the best quality mattresses, even in a top of the line hotel like this. We'll get a firm mattress for you when we get home."

"When are we going?" Quinn sat up, the blanket pooling around his hips. "Where are we going?"

"I live in my folks' house now. Dad died a year ago."

"I'm sorry to hear that." Quinn looked at her, his gaze intense. "How did he die?"

"His doctor diagnosed him with cancer a year after...I came home. He fought it as hard as he could but in the end it was too much. He's in Heaven now with Mom. After being apart for so many years I'm glad to know they're together again." Cassie shifted from one foot to the other knowing she had to tell Quinn the rest of what he'd missed while in captivity. "Your dad passed away too, Quinn."

Quinn's eyes closed for a second before flicking open again still expressionless. "When? How?"

"He had a heart attack about the same time my dad was diagnosed with cancer. He went quickly without any pain." Cassie rubbed a hand across her heart, remembering. Quinn's father had struggled a lot with the uncertainty of his son's situation. No one said for sure that it had caused his heart attack, but Cassie often wondered. And because Quinn's parents had been older when he and Renee had been born, their age had also been a factor in their health the past six years. "It was a rough time."

"And my mom?"

Cassie looked away from Quinn briefly, hating to have to give him more bad news. "She's in a nursing home. Renee tried to care for her after your dad's death, but it was too much."

Watching Esther's decline had been hard on Cassie. Having lost her own mom at an early age, Esther had filled that role in her life. It was like losing her mom all over again.

"What's wrong with her?" Even though there was no expression on Quinn's face it seemed it had become more starkly drawn in the past few minutes.

"She has Alzheimer's. She is doing well in the home, but there are days when she doesn't recognize any of us."

Quinn looked down. Cassie longed to wrap her arms around him and offer comfort but there was an invisible wall around him she couldn't breech. She settled instead for sitting down on the closed lid of the toilet, her hands gripping the album.

When Quinn looked up again she took a deep breath.

"Did you hear any of my messages?" Cassie asked.

Quinn's brow furrowed. "Messages?"

"Every year I made two messages that were broadcast over Colombian radio stations. In those messages I didn't give you the bad news, but I did give you some good." Cassie held out the album.

Quinn stared at it before reaching out and taking it from her. He flipped the cover open and when he saw the first picture he looked up quickly. For the first time since their reunion some emotion showed in his eyes. But it was there and gone so quickly Cassie couldn't tell for sure what it had been.

"What is this?" He looked down again at the picture that had been taken when Cassie was almost nine months pregnant. He didn't turn anymore pages.

"That special dinner I had planned for you the day you were taken had been to tell you I was pregnant."

"I have a..." Quinn flipped to the next page. "A daughter?"

"Yes. Janessa Quinn was born on April eight, the year after you were taken. She's five now and looking forward to meeting her daddy."

Quinn flipped through the album, pausing every so often to run a finger over a picture. The last picture in the album had been taken only days before hearing of his release. Cassie could picture it in her mind since she'd taken the time to slip the picture into the album less than twenty-four hours earlier. Jani's long brown curls hung to her waist and she was smiling, her brown eyes dancing so like the way Quinn's had before he'd…changed.

"She's beautiful," Quinn whispered hoarsely. "She looks like you."

"You think so?" Cassie cocked her head to one side. "I always thought she looked like you with her dark hair and eyes."

"Yes, but she smiles like you and the shape of her eyes are like yours."

Cassie felt her heart lighten. They had found a connection. Jani needed them both and they needed her to give them a focus for the future.

"Why did you name her Janessa Quinn?" Quinn had started back at the beginning of the album again.

"Well, the Quinn should be pretty obvious," Cassie said with a smile. "But Janessa I chose because of its meaning. I found out I was having a girl when I was seven months along. I'd been having a few contractions, and they wanted to make sure everything was okay, so they did an ultrasound. From that moment on I poured over the baby books looking for the right name. Janessa jumped out at me because it means God has been gracious."

Quinn glanced up at her, a questioning look on his face.

Cassie went on to explain, "When you were taken I was devastated. I didn't want to go on living because at first I was so sure they'd kill you. Knowing I had a baby depending on me helped to keep me going, and I knew that although you had been taken away, God had left a part of you with me. He was gracious in His gift of a daughter for me.

"She is what has kept me going, kept me alive in my heart and soul when I wanted to give up. I would look into her eyes and see you there and know I couldn't give up hope, that I couldn't stop praying and searching until we had some answers." Cassie smiled as she thought of their daughter. "We call her Jani for short, and she's anxious to meet you."

"Is she here in L.A.?" Quinn asked.

Cassie shook her head. "I decided to leave her at home with Renee. There is so much going on here I thought it was better to wait until we could go home. It was hard enough getting privacy for our own reunion. And I thought we might need a little time together first."

Quinn nodded slowly as he turned his attention back to the album. Cassie sat quietly watching him page through it for the third time. Again she was thankful for Jani's life. It had been hard telling Quinn about his parents, but at least she'd had some good news too.

"Can I keep this?" Quinn asked as he closed the album.

"Of course," Cassie replied readily. "I've been preparing that for you. We have many more pictures and videos at home. I've tried my best to chronicle Jani's life for you."

"Thank you." Quinn held the album to his chest.

An awkward silence filled the room. Uncomfortable with it, Cassie stood. "I'll let you get back to sleep. We have a press conference in the morning and then in the afternoon we're meeting with people from the mission. I've already told the guy in charge of the press conference that you may not wish to speak. I'll make a statement I've prepared but will not answer any questions right now."

"I'd rather not have to talk to the press," Quinn said with a frown.

"That's fine. I've actually become quite adept at dealing with them over the past six years. Last year I was on a nationwide documentary program with Mary Alice and Susan talking about our experiences."

"What about Emily? Why wasn't she there?" Quinn asked.

Cassie could see the worry in his eyes. "David was released and he's fine."

"Was he released recently?"

Cassie hesitated. In a way she hated to tell him how soon after they'd been taken that David had been freed. "No, not recently. They only kept him nine months."

Quinn's eyes widened. "Nine months? Why was he released so quickly?"

Cassie shrugged. "We don't know. Suddenly he ended up in Bogotá, sick but alive. David didn't know the language well enough to understand what was going on around him. It was a good thing though because at the check-up they gave him they discovered a suspicious patch on his skin. They diagnosed it as skin cancer, but because it was caught soon enough he got the treatment he needed and is now cancer free."

"And Kevin and Michael? The people I've been in contact with so far have been more interested in checking me over than giving me any information." Frustration laced Quinn's words.

"Up until this morning, you all were of the same status. We had no idea where you were or if you were still alive. Most reports we heard were that you were…dead." Sadness filled Cassie's heart. "I'm sure the news of your release is bittersweet for Mary Alice and Susan. It will give them hope that Kevin and Michael are still okay, but at the same time it's hard not to wish it were their husbands who had been released.

"I remember how I felt when I heard of David's release. It was hard because for the time immediately following his release I anticipated the call telling me you were free, too. I never imagined it would take six years." Cassie walked to the door of the bathroom, then turned back to look at Quinn. "I want you to know how glad I am to have you back. The thought of living the rest of my life without you was not something I wanted to contemplate."

Before Quinn could reply, Cassie left and headed back to her room.

*****

Quinn sat in the stillness of the bathroom, the album clutched tightly in his hands. He was still in shock. A daughter! It had been a big regret during the first few years of his captivity that he and Cassie had never had any kids. They had been trying before he'd been taken, but without success…or so he assumed. He'd known she'd make a terrific mom and apparently she had. Jani looked like a happy child.

With trembling fingers he opened the album again. He'd looked through it three times already but couldn't get enough of seeing Jani. He had missed so much. He wanted to ask God why but figured he wouldn't get any answers. Just as he hadn't gotten any for those years in the rebel camp until he was beyond hope and even caring.

Sadness seeped into his heart as Quinn looked at a picture of his dad holding Jani and His father wasn't waiting to welcome him home, and his mother might not even recognize him when they did meet again. At least he still had Renee. He wondered what his baby sister would think of the changes the past six years had brought. Something told him she wouldn't be too thrilled with some of them.

Quinn looked through the album a couple more times before hunkering back down on the bathroom floor and falling asleep.

Dreams, or rather nightmares, plagued him throughout the night. He woke each time sure he was actually back in the rebel camp dreaming about being free. Finally Quinn gave up any further attempt at sleeping.

Darkness still colored the city as he sat on the bed flipping the channels of the television. So much had happened while he'd been gone. A new president had taken up residence in the White house. Tragedies had hit the nation.

The world had gone on without him.

When the sky beyond the window began to lighten, Quinn turned off the television and started to prepare for what lay ahead. He left his room and went to the small fridge in the main part of the suite to find something to drink.

Ten minutes later Cassie came out of her room. She was dressed in a long black skirt and light pink blouse that skimmed her hips just a couple of inches below her waist. Her blond hair hung loose, shining in the morning sunlight. People never believed the blond was natural, but thanks to her Scandinavian background Cassie had never had to use a bottle of color on her hair.

Quinn remembered how much he had loved to see the way her hair sparkled in the sunshine. She had been his sunshine, always brightening his day with her look and her smile. A deep longing for the past filled Quinn. He wanted to go back. Back before the rebels had taken him. Back before the light and hope had faded from his life.

But even Cassie couldn't bring it back for him.

He cleared his throat. Cassie looked up from the piece of paper she was reading, a surprised look on her face. She paused momentarily but recovered quickly and approached him.

"Are you hungry?" she asked, picking up the room service menu. "I'm not really, but I know I should try and eat something. The press conference is set for ten."

"Just order me something simple. Some toast or pancakes."

Cassie nodded and picked up the phone to place the order. She had barely hung up the receiver when there was a knock on the door.

"Well, that can't be room service," Cassie said as she headed for the door.

Quinn followed behind her but stayed out of sight.

"Mr. Sidwell." Quinn heard Cassie say. "What are you doing here so early? I thought we'd see you just before the press conference."

"Yes, well I'd like to go over a few things before then."

"I'd prefer to wait until a little later," Cassie said firmly. "Quinn and I are going to have breakfast. We can meet you in an hour."

"I'd really rather go over this now," the man responded in a sharp voice.

"I believe my wife said later, Mr. Sidwell." Quinn moved to stand behind Cassie. He'd forgotten how short she was until that moment when he could look over the top of her head to the polished man standing in the doorway. "Your choices are to wait for an hour like Cassie requested, or forgo the conference all together."

"Uh no…" Sidwell took a step backward. "I'll be back in an hour."

He disappeared down the hallway as Cassie closed the door. She turned to him, a curious expression on her face. "I could have handled that."

"I know, but you never liked confrontational situations," Quinn reminded her.

"You're right, I don't, but I've learned how to stand my ground with bullies like him."

Quinn realized there were a few changes in Cassie he'd have to learn to deal with as well. "I'm sorry. I didn't mean to interfere."

A smile spread across Cassie's face. "That's okay. I appreciate the backup."

Another knock sounded at the door not long after. Cassie went to peek through the peephole before opening it. "Food!"

A uniformed man rolled the cart into the room, looking curiously at Quinn as he set up the table. Cassie tried to tip him but he brushed it aside and left them to their meal.

Quinn hadn't realized how hungry he was until the food arrived. He gladly ate all the pancakes and bacon Cassie had ordered for him.

"Would you like the rest of my omelet?" Cassie asked him, eyeing his empty plate.

"You didn't order it with onions, did you?"

Cassie shook her head. "Nope, no onions."

"In that case, I think I will finish it off for you. No sense in letting it go to waste."

"No sense at all," Cassie responded with a faint smile.

An hour on the dot brought another knock on the door and Mr. Sidwell was back.

"I've prepared a few questions Quinn can answer for the press."

Cassie took the list and read through it, shaking her head. "Quinn will not be speaking with the press. I have a prepared statement that I will give, but that's all we're prepared to do at the moment."

Sidwell began to sputter. "But...but...the press doesn't want a prepared statement. They want to talk to Quinn."

"That's just not going to be possible. Quinn will be there, of course, but he won't be answering any questions right now."

Quinn sat back watching Cassie at work. She'd been telling the truth when she'd said she could stand her ground. This time he didn't feel compelled to jump in and rescue her.

"The press will not be happy about this," Sidwell muttered under his breath.

"Well, then I guess that will make many unhappy people, myself included. Do you think I enjoy having to parade my private life out in public? The only reason I'm agreeing to do this is because many people across the country have been praying for Quinn's release and I want to thank them."

Sidwell was still muttering when the three of them left the suite five minutes later. Quinn marveled at Cassie's poise and calm manner. He remembered how she'd struggled as they travelled around the country, talking at different churches to raise financial support. She'd never enjoyed being the center of attention and speaking in public. It was obvious she'd come to terms with it though if she was this calm just before going on national television to speak to God only knew how many viewers.

A group of people rushed towards them as they approached the room where the press conference was taking place.

"You have three minutes before you go on," a man with a clipboard in one hand informed them. Someone else was there giving directions and talking with Cassie. Not sure what else to do, Quinn stuck close to her and took a deep breath when they were finally motioned out of the side room onto the stage to face the press.

*****

Cassie took several deep breaths trying to quell her nerves. Quinn sat next to her on the stage radiating tension which didn't help settle her nerves at all. She waited as Sidwell stood at the microphone first and said a few words. When he was done it was her turn. Taking a final deep breath, she placed her paper on the podium in front of her.

Cassie let her gaze drift across the crowd of reporters gathered in the small room. A few looked familiar, she'd seen them on television over the years.

"Thank you for coming today. Quinn and I would both like to thank the media for the coverage they have given his story. It has helped to spread the word to many people across this country and in turn, those people have joined many others worldwide in praying for Quinn's release.

"It has been a difficult six years of separation. Especially when we didn't know if Quinn was alive. I ask that you continue to pray for Kevin and Michael, the men who are still held captive, and their families. Quinn's release gives us hope they will be freed soon too.

"To have him home is wonderful. We are looking forward to some quiet time as a family. Time that will be spent getting reacquainted after such a long time apart.

"I hope you understand that our time in the spotlight has come to an end. Quinn is back home safe and sound, and now we need time to put our lives back together. We will be giving no further press conferences in the foreseeable future, and we will be unavailable to anyone but our closest friends and family.

"I want to take this opportunity to thank those across this country who have prayed faithfully for Quinn's release. God is good and in His time, He answered our prayers. Continue to pray for us as we go through an adjustment period." Cassie folded her paper and looked out at a crowd. "I am grateful to God that my husband is finally home again. This has been a difficult time for all of us close to the situation, and I am glad to know that this chapter of our lives is now closed.

"Thank you again for your support and understanding."

Cassie turned away from the podium, ignoring the clamor behind her as questions were shouted out. She knew the press was not happy to have to settle for a statement instead of being able to ask her and Quinn questions. The director of the mission was also present at the conference and would remain behind to field any questions the press had.

"Let's go." Quinn stood next to her.

Cassie looked up at him and nodded. "I'm ready for this to be over."

They made a quick exit and headed for the nearby elevators hoping to make their escape before the reporters started to follow them. A few other people joined them in the elevator but aside from a curious glance in their direction no one bothered them. Still, Cassie didn't breathe a sigh of relief until they were back in their suite with the door locked.

Cassie slumped down on the couch and slipped off her high heels. Leaning back she rotated her feet in circles, glad to have the shoes off. Cassie turned her head and saw Quinn pacing behind her, silhouetted by the sunlight streaming through the balcony door.

He paused and looked at her, his expression tense. "Are we going to have to stay here much longer?"

Cassie shifted so she could stretch her legs out on the couch and leaned an arm on the back of it. "I'm sorry, Quinn. I think we have to hang around a few more days. The mission, as well as the government people, want to talk to you. They want to offer you some counseling. And me too."

Quinn scowled and began to pace again. "I don't need counseling. I need to go home. I need to get away from all these people. I need to see my daughter."

Cassie didn't know what to say. She wanted him to take the counseling because she knew it would do them good. She'd been taking counseling off and on during the time he'd been gone. It helped so much to just be able to talk with someone. Cassie was sure he needed to have that outlet too even though he denied it.

"We'll talk to Ben Locke," Cassie said, referring to the mission director. "And see what he can do."

Quinn nodded and stopped for a moment to stare out the window before continuing to pace.

Cassie leaned her head back against the arm of the couch and closed her eyes. She felt a strong desire to call Emily to find out how to deal with all of Quinn's emotions. She'd gone through it when David had been released and perhaps could give her some advice. Of course David hadn't seemed as hardened as Quinn.

Cassie opened her eyes to look at her husband. It was like everything had hardened to stone in that jungle. His body, his heart, his soul.

A knock on the door interrupted her musings. Quinn turned from the window but Cassie waved a hand at him. "I'll get it."

As she had suspected, Ben Locke stood in the doorway.

"Hi Cassie, may I come in?"

"Sure, Ben. It's good to see you." The elderly man embraced Cassie before walking into the suite.

Ben held out his hand and shook Quinn's. "Good to see you again."

"You, too," Quinn replied in a stilted voice.

Ben turned back towards Cassie. "I just wanted to stop by and see how things are going. We'd like to have a meeting this afternoon with Quinn, if that's okay. A debriefing, if you will."

Cassie glanced at Quinn and saw his jaw clench. "We were just talking about that. How long do you think it will be before we can go home?"

Ben looked at Quinn, then back to Cassie. "We'd like to have a few days with you both. I understand you're anxious to get home, but I think it would be a good idea for you to take advantage of the help that is being offered."

"I'll go to the meeting, the debriefing, this afternoon," Quinn said. "But then I'd like to go home. This evening if possible, tomorrow at the latest. I'm sure Cassie has people who can help us there as well as here."

"I really don't recommend leaving so soon," Ben said, his brow furrowed.

"I appreciate your concern but right now I have some concerns of my own. My mother isn't doing well, she's the only parent I still have, and then there's my daughter whom I've never met. I want to go home."

Ben looked at Cassie, pleading in his eyes. Cassie just shrugged. She understood Quinn's desire to see his mom and Jani, she wanted to see them, too.

"There's no way I can change your mind?" Ben asked.

Quinn shook his head. "For too long I've had to bend to the wishes of others. I'm free now and this is my decision. I want to be home with my family."

Ben nodded. "Okay. I'll call those we are to meet with this afternoon and let you know what time the debriefing will be. Why don't you grab some lunch?"

Cassie walked Ben to the door. Surprisingly, he left without asking her to try to change Quinn's mind. Cassie closed the door but lingered with her hand on the handle. She leaned her forehead against the smooth wood and closed her eyes.

"God, please help me. Quinn seems so hard, so different than the man I married. I don't know what to say, what to do. Give me wisdom and understanding. Please don't let my family fall apart."

Taking a deep breath, Cassie pushed away from the door and went back to the living room. Quinn stood, head bent, looking at the room service menu. He looked up as she walked towards him.

"Have you decided what you'd like for lunch?" she asked as he handed her the menu.

Within half an hour they were eating their lunch, waiting for Ben's call. Cassie's appetite had vanished but she forced herself to eat knowing it was going to be a long afternoon. She only hoped that it was a positive experience and not a negative one.

Chapter Three

Cassie pushed the snaps shut on her small suitcase and heaved it off the bed, grunting. It hit the floor with a muffled thud and fell onto its side. She just stared at it, exhaustion dragging at her body.

The past day had been jam packed with meetings. She and Quinn barely had any time together. Once they finished their lunch Ben returned and they headed off for the first of Quinn's debriefings. Cassie hadn't participated in those meetings but met with a counselor instead. Quinn's meetings ran long so Cassie had spent some time with Cecily talking and praying.

By the time they'd gotten back to the hotel it had been late, and Cassie could tell Quinn was in no mood for conversation. They'd gone straight to bed and even though she had been wiped out, Cassie had struggled to fall asleep.

Now she was paying for it.

Wearily Cassie picked up the suitcase and headed for the door of the bedroom. She spotted Quinn standing at the window looking out at the smog-filled sky. It seemed he spent a lot of time staring out the window. Almost as if he longed to be out of the building, out of the confines of the hotel.

He turned when she bumped the suitcase against the wall.

"Let me get that for you," he said and came towards her.

Dark circles lay beneath Quinn's eyes and he appeared even gaunter than he had the day before. He looked as tired as she felt. It was a good thing they were heading home. They both needed some rest.

She sat down on the couch as Quinn carried the suitcase over to the hallway where he'd put his duffle bag. It was tempting to close her eyes to try and get a bit more sleep, but she doubted she'd actually fall asleep with Quinn so near, even if she had the time.

"How much longer till we're out of here?" Quinn prowled restlessly around the room.

"Aaron and Cecily said they would be coming by to pick us up. I expect they'll arrive in the next little while. Our plane leaves in three hours." Cassie couldn't help smiling as she thought about Aaron and Cecily. They had been a great support to her over the past few years and had become close friends.

There was a knock at the door. Cassie moved to stand but Quinn waved her back. "I'll get it."

Cassie didn't argue. Closing her eyes, she sank back against the couch. When she heard Sidwell's nasal voice greet Quinn, she stifled a groan.

"We'd like to talk with you and your wife."

"I'm afraid that's not possible. We did your press conference but now we'd like some time to ourselves."

"But we've lined up an interview." He went on to mention a top name journalist and documentary program. "They will come by later this afternoon to meet with you and then start filming tomorrow."

"That won't work. We're leaving."

Even from a distance Cassie could hear the impatience in Quinn's voice. He used to be much more diplomatic and patient. Of course Sidwell was as annoying as a mosquito buzzing around, and she lost her patience with him as well. Sometimes it felt like she was talking to a brick wall whenever she tried to hold a conversation with the man.

Over the years he had been the representative from the government she'd had to deal with. He'd lined up interviews before and Cassie had to admit he'd help to get the word out about Quinn and the others, if only he wasn't so annoying.

"You're…you're leaving?" Sidwell sputtered.

"I'm sorry but our public life has come to an end. We need privacy now."

Cassie heard the soft click as the door shut and grinned. She could just imagine Sidwell standing on the other side, glaring at it.

Quinn came back into the room as Cassie opened her eyes. He had a frown on his face. "That man is a pain."

"Yes, he's been a pain for the past three years. Hasn't changed much at all. Well, he got a little worse when he was promoted."

With a shake of his head, Quinn dropped into the chair across from her. "I hope your friends show up soon. I can't handle being holed up in this hotel room for very much longer." His head bent forward until his chin rested on his chest.

Her earlier observation about him feeling cooped up in the hotel room, spacious though it was, had been right. It made her doubly glad for the plans she had made now that she realized how much Quinn disliked being confined.

"When we get home we're going to pick Jani up and head for the cabin."

Quinn's head lifted. "We're going out to the cabin?"

"Yes, I figured it was the best place to go. Peace and quiet, and lots of fresh air and privacy."

Cassie looked closely at Quinn, dismayed to see the lines of tension on his face had not eased at all since she'd first seen him. A wave of emotion swept over her. She longed to go to him, curl up in his lap and offer him comfort. They had done that a lot in the past. It was a wonderful way to end the day, curled up together, talking and sharing. Quinn had held her many times as she'd cried from homesickness when they'd first arrived in South America.

Tears formed in Cassie's eyes. Quickly she blinked and looked away from Quinn. The memories of the past had been all that had kept her going over the years, now they only caused pain as the realization came that things would never be like that again. Both she and Quinn had changed so much.

Too much? Cassie wondered.

"I think I'll just go check over the room once more to make sure I didn't leave anything." Cassie stood, suddenly eager to be alone.

Quinn nodded. "I'll do the same. The sooner we can get out of here the better."

Within half an hour the knock they'd both been waiting for sounded. Cassie checked the peephole before opening the door and embracing Aaron and Cecily.

"I'm so glad to see you guys," Cassie said as she stepped back to let them into the room.

"Been a rough couple of days?" Aaron asked.

Cassie shrugged. "Dealing with all the bureaucracy is a pain. Even the mission, I hate to say. I know it's for our own good but I just want to get on with life."

Aaron shook Quinn's hand when he joined them. "Everything okay?"

"It's going to be once we get out of here." Quinn picked up his bag. "Is it time to go?"

Aaron hesitated for a moment. "Are you sure you're ready? I really think you should reconsider the counseling the mission is offering."

Quinn sighed and dropped his bag back onto the carpet. "I talked to a counselor already. Two of them, in fact, managed to find room for me in their no-doubt busy schedule yesterday."

Cassie tried to keep her jaw from dropping. She had never heard Quinn speak so sarcastically before. It struck a chord of fear within her. Just how much had Quinn changed?

"Two sessions aren't enough, Quinn," Aaron said calmly. "You need something more long-term. Involving Cassie."

Cassie looked from Quinn to Aaron. Tension was thick and getting thicker. She had never, ever, sensed such a tension in Quinn in all the years she had known him.

"Aaron, I have a counselor at home," Cassie said, hoping to cool things down. "I'll give her a call."

Aaron nodded. "Do, Cassie. I think it's very important. In talking to David Warner it's been the one thing that helped him after his release."

It bothered Cassie to see the looks of concern on Aaron and Cecily's faces. They'd become so close to her over the years and she hated to see them so worried. "Don't worry, Aaron, I'll take care of it."

"Well, then, I guess it's time to get you guys off to the airport."

Relieved, Cassie picked up her purse and followed the men and Cecily out the door. A bellhop stood waiting to take their bags down to the lobby. Within fifteen minutes they had checked out and were on their way to the airport.

Aaron and Cecily came into the airport terminal with them. Since there was time before their flight left, they decided to have a quick coffee.

*****

Quinn stared at the crush of people walking within the airport. Everywhere he looked there were people. More people than he had seen in the past six years. Combined.

Plane arrival and departure announcements blared over the speakers, interrupting the elevator music that played. It was a cacophony of noise to Quinn's ears.

Quinn shifted on the padded seat. He tried to push aside the longing for the solitude and peace and quiet of the jungle but it was there and couldn't be ignored. He hoped it was just the shocking comparison of coming from the jungle to a chaotic city like LA and that it would pass as he got used to being back among people.

A hand touched his arm.

"Quinn?"

Looking away from the crowds, Quinn saw concern in Cassie's eyes.

"Are you okay?" she asked.

Quinn nodded, wondering how many times he was going to hear that question. "Just anxious to get home."

"Another few hours and we'll be there. We'll take my car to Renee's house. She said she'll have everything ready for us to go to the cabin."

Relief eased some of the tension from Quinn. He was glad to finally be leaving behind the three-ring circus he'd been a part of since his release.

"Did you want to see your mom before we head out to the cabin?" Cassie asked.

Quinn glanced back at the people walking by. "Will she know I'm there?"

"It depends on the day. Sometimes she remembers but those days are becoming fewer and fewer. Unfortunately."

"I'd like to wait a little while longer. I don't want her to see me like this. I need to just…relax."

"We can go after our time up at the cabin, or sooner if you feel up to it."

Quinn nodded but remained silent.

By the time they had finished their coffee it was time to board the plane. Aaron and Cecily walked with them as far as security.

"We'll be praying for you both and Jani too as you settle in," Aaron said. He hugged Cassie. "If you need anything, anything at all, please call."

"I will." Cassie moved to hug Cecily. "You're on my speed dial."

Quinn took Cassie's bag from Aaron and they walked through security.

They spent most the flight in silence. What they needed to talk about wasn't suitable conversation for a plane trip and there just wasn't any small talk Quinn could come up with. He wanted the flight to be over and to finally meet his daughter. It couldn't be soon enough.

To help pass the time, Quinn read the newspapers the stewardess had offered, eager to learn everything he could about what had happened while he had been out of touch with the rest of the world.

*****

Cassie was glad when the plane finally touched down at the Twin Cities airport. Thankfully their bags were among the first to begin the trip around the baggage carousel so it wasn't long before they left the terminal.

A rush of cool, damp air greeted them as they walked out of the building. Dark clouds obscured the sunshine and they had to walk around puddles that lay on the sidewalk. Though it was still technically summer, the day held a moist chill from the cloudy rainy sky.

Cassie led the way to where she'd left her SUV in the long-term parking. She was glad to get inside, sheltered from the cold wind.

They had about an hour's trip ahead of them depending on traffic. As Cassie had anticipated, Quinn remained silent but this time she didn't. "Jani is so excited to meet you. She knows all about you and has looked forward to this moment for as long as she has understood why you weren't home."

Quinn looked at her. "But you told her all about the person I was. I'm a different person now."

Pain lanced through Cassie's heart. She knew it was true but to hear him actually say the words hurt. "She'll still love you, Quinn. You're her daddy, no matter how you've changed."

Without saying anything more, Quinn turned toward the side window. Cassie kept her gaze on the road and her hands clenched on the wheel. Was there anything she could do to make this easier for Quinn and Jani? She just wanted Jani to have her daddy and for Quinn to have his daughter. For them to be a family.

Cassie didn't bother to pursue conversation for the rest of the trip. It was too emotional to deal with when her attention was divided. She breathed a sigh of relief when she finally turned onto Renee's street.

"We're here," she said softly, turning the vehicle into the driveway.

She climbed out and waited for Quinn. Together they headed for the front door. She'd asked Renee to keep Jani inside so their first meeting was out of sight of any prying eyes that might be lurking around.

Cassie reached for the doorbell, closing her eyes to say a quick prayer just before she pressed it. How badly she wanted this to go well. For all their sakes.

The door swung open, and Cassie got a glimpse of her sister-in-law's eager face. She stepped into the hallway and passed Renee so Quinn could follow. The door closed and as Cassie turned, she saw Renee throw herself into brother's arms. There was no hesitation on Quinn's part as he wrapped his arms around his sister and buried his face in her hair.

Cassie reached out a hand to the wall. Her heart clenched with pain as she watched them. He'd had no such embrace for her. And this embrace was lasting far longer than theirs had.

Afraid she would burst into tears, Cassie left them alone in the hall. She dropped her purse on a chair in the living room before heading up to the bedroom where Jani usually stayed. She had asked Renee to let her talk with Jani first before introducing her to Quinn.

The door to the room was open, and Cassie could see her small daughter standing next to the window. She had probably seen them arrive since the window faced the front street.

"Hi, sweetheart," Cassie said softly.

Jani spun around and darted across the room to throw herself into Cassie's embrace. Holding her daughter tightly, Cassie drew some comfort in knowing that even if her husband didn't love her, her daughter did.

"I missed you so much, Mama." Jani lifted her face for Cassie's kiss.

Cassie smoothed a few loose strands of hair from her small face. "I missed you too. More than you'll ever know." Keenly aware that Quinn was waiting downstairs, Cassie dropped to her knees in front of Jani. "You know your daddy's here, right?"

Jani nodded, her eyes wide.

"He's waiting downstairs to meet you. Are you ready to meet him?"

After the slightest hesitation, Jani nodded.

Cassie stood and took her daughter's hand. Slowly they left the room and descended the stairs to meet the stranger who was Jani's father.

*****

Quinn sat on the edge of the soft couch in Renee's living room. His heart pounded with the anticipation of meeting his daughter for the first time.

"She's been so anxious to meet you, Quinn. She's talked of nothing else since Cassie left the other day."

"I'm anxious too but a little worried. I'm not the same person you and Cassie knew six years ago. What if Jani doesn't like who I am?"

"She will," Renee stated confidently. "You're her daddy and that's all that matters."

Movement at the doorway of the living room drew Quinn's attention. Cassie stood there with a little girl at her side.

"Jani, this is your daddy," Cassie said softly. With a hand on Jani's back she moved toward Quinn.

Quinn looked into Jani's eyes and saw no fear, just an assessing look as she took him in.

"Hi, Jani. I'm glad to finally meet you."

Jani's head cocked to the side for a moment and then straightened. "Your hair's different."

Quinn lifted a hand to his cropped hair. "Yes, it was easier to have it short like this. Do you mind?"

Jani smiled and shook her head. Tentatively she took a step toward him but Quinn made no move to reach out to draw her close. He wanted her to feel perfectly comfortable with him and for her to be the one to make the first move.

"Are you home forever?" she asked.

"I certainly hope so. If I leave again, I'll be taking you with me."

"And Mommy too?"

Quinn hesitated, wishing he had the reassurances Jani wanted. He didn't want to lie to her but he also didn't want to get into what the future held just yet. "And Mommy too."

Seeming satisfied with his answers, Jani approached him until she stood next to his knee. Quinn held his breath as she reached out and stroked his cheek with her hand.

"My friend's daddy holds her on his lap. Will you do that too?"

"If that's what you want." Quinn finally made a move of his own and reach out to touch her soft curls. "Would you like me to hold you now?"

Jani nodded and raised her arms so he could lift her onto his knee. As he lifted her, Quinn was instantly reminded of just how much time he'd lost with his daughter. The first time a father held his child should be as an infant, not as a five-year old. Bitterness filled his throat.

He hadn't held her just moments after she'd taken her first breath. He hadn't been able to cuddle her close and smell that special baby smell. He hadn't seen her roll over for the first time or when she'd been cranky while cutting her first tooth. He hadn't been the one to catch and encourage her as she'd taken her first tentative steps. He'd missed so much.

God, why couldn't you have answered my prayers sooner? You knew I had a daughter waiting at home for me. Did she deserve to spend the past five years without her father?

Quinn knew then wasn't the time or the place to let his bitterness flow. He tamped it down and tried to concentrate on the beautiful, sweet smelling little girl he held in his arms.

He was vaguely aware of Cassie leaving the room although Renee stayed, encouraging Jani to tell him about different things in her life.

Within five minutes Quinn knew his daughter loved chocolate and broccoli but hated green beans and carrots. She knew how to ride a bike but still had to have the "baby wheels" as she called them. She loved to draw but had gotten in trouble for coloring on the wall of her room.

Quinn held her close. Suddenly he was eager to get to the cabin and learn even more about his daughter. He stood, still holding Jani in his arms. "I think we'd better go, Renee. We still have a couple hours to go to get to the cabin."

Renee nodded and smiled ruefully. "I really hate to see you go so soon but I understand. Maybe I'll come up on Sunday."

"That would be great."

"I'll just go get Cassie. Everything is packed and ready to go. It's all in the garage just waiting to be loaded."

Cassie met them in the hallway leading to the garage. "Do you need to go to the bathroom before we leave, Jani?"

Jani nodded. Quinn relinquished her to Cassie so she could take care of business before they left.

Fifteen minutes later they were on their way. Quinn wished he could have driven but realized it was impossible since he didn't have a valid driver's license. Instead he took the passenger seat of the SUV and turned so he could see Jani where she sat just behind Cassie.

Jani smiled at him, a wide-open grin. Quinn couldn't help but respond even though the muscles of his face protested the action. Smiling hadn't been something he'd done an awful lot of over the past few years.

Not long into their trip Jani's head began to bob and soon she was sound asleep with her head against the side of her seat. Quinn watched her for a while longer before turning his attention away from Jani. His gaze settled on Cassie, and he sensed a shift in her mood from earlier.

Her face seemed a little paler than it had been and there was tightness around her eyes and mouth he didn't recall seeing before. Clearly something was bothering her. At one time he would have asked and then cajoled it out of her but this time he just turned his attention to the scenery outside the window. He didn't have the energy to deal with it.

Quinn didn't want to think about Cassie and their marriage. It had been great to see Renee and they had fallen right back into their brother-sister relationship. Things with Jani were great and could only get better as far as Quinn was concerned, but he didn't know what to do about his relationship with Cassie.

Renee loved him because he was her brother and that relationship was there no matter what. Jani loved him because he was the father she'd always wanted. But Cassie...

How could he expect her to love him when he didn't know if he could ever return the feelings? He wasn't the man she'd married nine years ago. He wasn't the man she'd fallen in love with. How on earth could they just pick up where they'd left off as if nothing had happened? And if they weren't just going to pick up, where did they start?

Quinn had no answers for his own questions and somehow he doubted Cassie did either. The scariest part for Quinn was thinking that perhaps he could never love that way again. His hostage ordeal had killed a lot of what he'd held dear six years ago. His love for Cassie and his faith in God.

One he wasn't sure he'd ever get back and the other he wasn't sure he wanted to get back. But if he could find that love for Cassie again, could she accept him even if he didn't share her faith in God? Somehow Quinn didn't think she'd understand. At that moment it just seemed easiest to think about his relationships with Renee and Jani. They were straightforward and uncomplicated, and that was what he needed very badly.

Surely Cassie could wait another few weeks before they started working on their own relationship. It would give them time to get to know each other again and to find out what they wanted from each other. Quinn just hoped Cassie wouldn't ask for more before he was ready because he just wasn't sure he had it within himself to give.

He glanced over at her and again the bitterness began to rise. Why had God allowed him to be robbed of so many precious things? He had gone to the mission field prepared to serve God there for the rest of his life, but God had repaid his faithfulness by abandoning him for almost six years.

Quinn didn't think he could forgive God for that. He had lost too much. Most of which he'd never again regain. That chapter of his life was closed. It was time to move on. Without God and possibly without Cassie. He didn't like to think about life without Cassie but he had to face reality and that reality was that Cassie probably wouldn't want a relationship with him if she knew just how much of his faith he had lost.

Quinn wasn't sure he would ever again search after God with his whole heart. Not even for Cassie.

Trying to push aside the overwhelming thoughts, Quinn picked up the bundle of papers and magazines Renee had handed him as they walked out of the house. Again he drank in the news and information they contained. His attention and emotions were being pulled in so many different directions. Quinn felt he would never get a grasp on everything.

Chapter Four

"Do you want something to eat?" Cassie asked, briefly taking her gaze from the straight stretch of road in front of them. "Renee packed us a cooler of stuff since we arrived right at supper time."

Quinn shook his head. "I'm not terribly hungry. I'll grab a bite when we get to the cabin."

He turned his attention back to the paper and silence once again filled the interior of the car.

Cassie took a deep breath then forced the air out past tense lips, relaxing her grip on the steering wheel. Tension still hung thick and heavy in the SUV. Part of her wanted to fill the tense silence with conversation about something, anything, but Quinn sat silent beside her, his head buried in a newspaper. And the bottom line was she had no idea what to talk to Quinn about. So much had changed in six years.

The sun set as Cassie maneuvered the vehicle along the now winding road that led to the cabin, thankful the long summer evening had provided light for most the trip. She breathed a sigh of relief when she finally pulled the vehicle to a stop in front of the cabin that had been in her dad's family for several generations. She quickly stepped out, leaving the headlights on to illuminate the way to the cabin since there were no streetlights out this far.

"Why don't I carry her," Quinn suggested as he came around the side of the SUV where she stood, opening Jani's door. "She's probably a bit heavy for you."

Cassie started to remind him she'd managed just fine for the past six years lifting Jani by herself but she held her tongue. That reminder would serve no purpose but to increase the already tense situation between them. She stepped aside so Quinn could lean in and lift the tiny girl into his arms.

Cassie hurried ahead of him and climbed the rough-hewn wooden steps to the porch of the cabin. She unlocked the front door and pushed it open, fumbling for the switch. Light flooded the room just as Quinn stepped through the doorway.

"Can you hold her a minute while I go turn off the headlights and get her bed made up?" Cassie asked, glancing towards the door leading off the living room.

Quinn nodded and slowly sank into one of the armchairs near the fireplace. Cassie hurried out to the SUV, flipping on the porch light as she went. Once she'd turned the vehicle off, Cassie returned to the cabin. She went to the closet in the bedroom and pulled down the box that held the bedding for the cabin. She made quick work of the single bed before calling Quinn to bring Jani in. Cassie decided to not try to change Jani out of her sweat suit since the nights could be cool anyway and she didn't want to waken her.

Once Quinn placed Jani on the bed Cassie covered her with the blanket, then switched on the small lamp on the night table. She turned off the bright overhead light as they left the room.

"I'll get the bags from the car," Quinn said as he strode towards the front door.

Cassie didn't bother to argue with him, instead she went into the small kitchen to turn on the refrigerator. The cabin at one time had been smaller and more rustic but over the years upgrades and additions had been added on. Cassie loved the cabin. It held lots of happy memories for her.

She pushed aside lacy, cotton sky-blue curtains to look out the small window over the sink towards the lake. The moon was nearly full and its reflection moved like molten gold as the water rippled in the light evening breeze. Before she could stop it, her mind drifted back to another night, another full moon.

They'd spent their honeymoon at the cabin. Most evenings they had wandered down to the dock and lay there looking up at the sky and the wondrous myriad of stars barely visible in the city but sparkling with diamond beauty in the dark country night.

Words of love and affection had been whispered even though they were the only ones around for miles. It had been as if they'd not even wanted to share what existed between them with the creatures of the forest and the nature that surrounded them. It had been just the two of them. Closer to each other than they'd been with any other person before.

Cassie reached out a hand towards the lake, stopping when her fingers brushed the cold, hard glass of the window. But even as her hand stopped, her memories did not.

"I'll love you forever, Sunshine," Quinn whispered, the warmth of his breath caressing her ear. "Even when we're old and gray, we'll still come here and lie on the dock to watch the stars. I'll hold you in my arms and tell you that even after all the years, I still love you."

Cassie's heart swelled with love for the man who held her. God had blessed her the perfect match for her heart. She would never be happier than when he held her in his arms. "I love you too, Quinn. More than you'll ever know."

"Cassie, my love..." Their lips met in a gentle kiss. "My darling Cassie..."

"Cassie?"

Startled, Cassie dropped her hand from the window and struggled to control herself before turning to face Quinn. Maybe coming to the cabin had been a big mistake. At one time the memories had brought her joy and happiness, a warmth and an anticipation of what the future held when Quinn returned. This time they left her feeling empty, hollowed out of everything, including hope.

"You'll have to tell me where you want this stuff," Quinn told her, gesturing to the pile of bags near the doorway.

Cassie nodded and moved out of the kitchen alcove. She didn't look at Quinn as she approached the bags. "Mine and Jani's can go in Jani's room. You can have the loft. Any boxes probably have food in them so they, along with the cooler, can go right into the kitchen. I'll go finish making up the beds."

Closing her mind to the past, Cassie got the set of sheets for the bed in the loft. Her feet felt weighted as she climbed the stairs to the large open loft area. A big picture window filled one wall and the moonlight gave almost sufficient light for her to make the bed. But Cassie didn't want to make the bed in a room lit only by moonlight. It brought back memories of times they'd spent together in that loft, that bed, bathed in moonlight.

Cassie hit the light switch with more force than necessary and was relieved when the harsh light dispelled the soft moonlight. If only memories could be dispelled as easily.

Quickly pulling the sheets into place, Cassie tried hard to ignore the trembling of her hands. *It just wasn't fair,* her mind raged. Tonight she should have been sharing the loft with Quinn. They should have been wrapped in each other's arms and the love they shared but instead she'd be sleeping in a narrow bed downstairs…alone.

Thankfully Quinn didn't come up there while she made the bed. Cassie didn't think she could handle her memories and him together in the loft. She left as soon as she finished making the bed and retreated downstairs. She saw boxes sitting on the counter in the kitchen and headed there to begin unpacking them.

Quinn came out of the room where Jani slept. "Are you sure you want to sleep on that bed?"

Cassie's breath snagged in her lungs. What was he suggesting? "It will be fine."

"I can sleep on the couch and you could have the loft. You'd probably be more comfortable."

Cassie stared down at the can of pork and beans she held in her hand, the label swimming beneath her watery gaze. How many times in the months ahead would she get her hopes up only to have them smacked down?

"I'll be fine." She turned without looking at Quinn and stuck the can in the cupboard.

There was not enough money on the earth to pay her to sleep in the loft with Quinn in the same cabin, sleeping on the couch. In the past six years she had willingly slept in the loft even though it had been hard the first few times. The memories had brought her comfort and in the darkest moments of despair she had clung to them and allowed herself to dream of the future. Now that future lay shattered at her feet.

Cassie didn't think she had the strength to lie in that bed and not spend the whole night in tears. It didn't appear Quinn would have the same problem.

Half an hour later the kitchen boxes had been emptied. Cassie rotated her shoulders and rolled her head, trying to ease the weariness of her body. The emotions that filled her now were very reminiscent of the ones she'd gone through when Quinn had first been taken hostage. Despair, grief, anger. The list went on and on. Last time there had been some hope but that night Cassie just wasn't sure if any hope remained for their future. Quinn was so distant with her. Not with his sister, not with Jani, only with her.

Cassie took a deep breath to try to control the pain. She couldn't fall apart yet. She couldn't let Quinn see the pain that had overtaken her. At one time he would have taken her into his arms and held her, whispering soothing words of comfort in her ear. But Cassie was afraid that now he'd see her pain and turn away. She wasn't sure if she could survive that.

She heard the pipes creak as Quinn turned on the water in the upper bathroom. She finished emptying the cooler Renee had made for them. Even though she hadn't eaten since earlier in the day, Cassie wasn't hungry. She figured anything she ate just wouldn't sit well with her stomach.

Cassie shoved the empty boxes and cooler into the small pantry and headed for her room. Jani lay sprawled, sound asleep on the opposite bed. Cassie stared down at her little daughter and thanked God for giving Jani to her. Once again, Jani would be her reason for continuing on. She would be strong for her. Cassie would do her best to try and make whatever situation Quinn wanted to work…for Jani's sake. Her daughter was the most important thing right now.

Cassie brushed aside a tendril of hair from Jani's cheek and pressed a soft kiss to her satin skin. Oh, for the sleep of an innocent child. Cassie didn't think her slumber that night would be as peaceful or as deep as Jani's.

Turning away, Cassie focused on their bags. Moving quietly she began to unpack them, putting their things in the chest of drawers that stood against the wall.

She heard the water shut off and then Quinn's footsteps as he walked into the loft. He moved around for a while then the cabin fell silent.

Cassie finished unpacking and took the sweat suit she planned to sleep in to the bathroom with her. She took a quick shower and changed, turning off the lights as she made her way back to her room. She glanced at the stairs to the loft from which glowed a soft light. They hadn't even said goodnight.

Back in her own bed, Cassie said a brief prayer and tried to fall asleep.

Unfortunately, it didn't come and finally Cassie gave up. She left the bedroom and with a knowledge born of many nights spent in the cabin, Cassie avoided the squeaky boards in the floor as she made her way to the front door. She found her jacket and slipped her feet into shoes she'd left by the door earlier and headed out of the cabin.

Cassie started to head for the dock but veered off and instead went to the large rock that jutted out over the water. Following a path illuminated by the moonlight, Cassie made her way to the rock and climbed up onto it.

The cool, hard surface of the rock greeted her as she sat down. Cassie bent her knees and pulled them close to her chest, chin resting on them. With weary eyes she stared out across the water.

Nature sang its chorus all around her and serenity filled the air. Cassie longed for the same serenity in her soul. Instead emotions she didn't want to have to deal with filled her heart.

What was she going to do? With every passing hour she spent in Quinn's presence it became more and more apparent he didn't want things the way they used to be. But what did he want?

Cassie was too afraid to ask. Too afraid because it might mean all her dreams would be broken beyond repair. Dreams of being a family again. Dreams of adding to their family. She longed for another baby. This time she wanted to go through her pregnancy with Quinn by her side. It didn't look like that was going to happen.

The golden moonlight blurred, and Cassie blinked. Against the cool of the evening air, the tear that slid down her cheek felt scalding. She brushed it away but another soon followed. And then another. Finally she gave in to the agony in her heart.

She lowered her forehead onto her arms and let her grief spill out.

*****

Quinn shifted restlessly on the bed. Unlike the previous nights, unfamiliarity with the bed did not cause all his restlessness. As soon as he'd turned off the light, moonlight and memories flooded him.

They were memories he didn't want to deal with. Memories he didn't know how to deal with. A different man had made those memories. What was he supposed to do with them? He couldn't shove them aside as easily as he had in the past few days. The memories in his mind now were vivid and full of emotion.

Quinn swung his feet over the side of the bed and stood. There was no way he could get any sleep in that bed tonight. The floor would be just fine.

He picked up the pillow and blanket and tossed them on the floor. Instead of lying right down, Quinn found himself drawn to the large window through which the moonlight spilled. He planned to pull the curtains to darken the room and hopefully remove the atmosphere that was creating unwanted memories. As he reached for the edge of the curtain his gaze fell on a huddled figure on the large rock near the water's edge.

Cassie.

What was she doing out there at that time of night? He hadn't even heard her leave the cabin.

Quinn moved closer to the window and watched her sitting there, head bent and shoulders hunched. Part of him, a part he'd thought long dead, suddenly longed to go to her. To hold her close and comfort her. But how could he comfort her when he was the source of all her pain? And how could he comfort her when he couldn't offer her what she wanted? Her husband back.

Quinn suppressed the urge to smash his hand against the glass. Anger coursed through him for all he'd lost.

Minutes passed and still he stood there. And still Cassie sat motionless on the rock. Finally her head lifted and she stared out across the lake. She rubbed a hand across her cheek and Quinn assumed it was to rub away tears she had shed.

He watched as she slowly stood and moved off the rock. His gaze followed her progress through the moonlight. At one point she glanced up at the window and paused. Quinn didn't think she could see him but still he stepped to the side, out of the wash of moonlight. Her head lowered and she continued her walk back to the cabin. This time he heard her moving around downstairs.

As Quinn stood there he knew he owed Cassie some sort of idea of what he viewed the future holding for them. The longer he held off, the more likely she was to get her hopes up about things working out between them. Little did she know how unlikely that was.

Maybe once she knew the depth of his failure and lack of his faith she'd understand. But could he bare his soul so completely? At one time he would have told Cassie anything. But now everything had changed.

Quinn glanced out the window one last time. *Everything*.

*****

"Mama! Mama!" Cassie woke to Jani's impatient voice. "Is my daddy still here?"

Cassie rolled over to face her daughter. "Yes, Sweetheart, he's still here. He's sleeping in the loft."

"Can I see him?"

With a sigh, Cassie sat up, all hope of sleeping in pretty much gone. "I don't know if he's awake yet. Why don't you go out quietly and see if he's in the living room. But don't go upstairs in case he still wants to sleep."

Jani nodded and quickly left the room.

Cassie swung her legs over the side of the bed, slipped her hands under her thighs and stared down at her toes. She didn't want to face the day, didn't want to face Quinn but hiding wouldn't help any.

Resolutely she stood and made their beds. Before leaving the room she changed into a pair of jeans and a loose sweater and ran a brush through her hair.

As soon as she opened the door she heard voices and knew Quinn was awake already.

"Can you make pancakes?" Cassie heard Jani ask.

"I used to make them but it's been a while. I think you'd be better off waiting for your mom."

Cassie remembered well the pancakes he'd brought to her the morning after their wedding. He'd covered them with whipped cream and strawberries. They had been absolutely scrumptious.

More memories. Would they ever end?

"Hi, Mama!" Jani skipped towards her. "Can I have pancakes for breakfast? Daddy said you should make them and not him."

"Your dad makes great pancakes but I don't mind making them for you this morning." Cassie chanced a glance at Quinn, wondering if he had the same memory as she did of that morning.

Quinn's eyes narrowed, his gaze hardening. Cassie looked away. She wanted to see joy in his eyes at the memories, not hardness. Just another reality she had to face. Quinn didn't want to dwell on the past, didn't want to regain the past. What did that mean for their future?

"Can I help you make them?" Jani asked, already digging through the cupboard for a bowl.

"If you'd like." Grateful for the distraction, Cassie moved to help Jani get the ingredients together.

Cassie heard the front door close and looked up to find Quinn gone. She looked out the window and saw him heading for the dock.

When the pancakes were done she sent Jani out to get him while she poured the coffee. Quinn came back holding Jani's hand and listening intently to her chatter.

Once they were seated Jani bowed her head and immediately began to pray. Cassie, a little slow to respond, noted that Quinn was even slower.

Their pancakes that morning were served simply with butter and syrup. Cassie wished she had brought cream and strawberries to go with them. Part of her just longed to shove their memories in Quinn's face. Maybe then he'd quit acting like none of it ever happened. Maybe then he'd realize they had something worth fighting for.

"Do you play checkers, Daddy?" Jani asked as she finished off her first pancake.

"I've played a game or two in my life," Quinn replied with a nod.

"Will you play with me?" Jani leaned forward eagerly. "Mama isn't a very good player. Auntie Renee taught me and now I can beat Mama."

"I used to play checkers with your Aunt Renee a lot when we were younger. I hope she didn't teach you to cheat."

Jani just looked at him, a questioning expression on her face. "Cheat?"

"I don't think Renee has gotten to that lesson yet," Cassie said with a small grin. "Probably wants her to get the finer points of the game down before teaching her to cheat."

"You never bothered with the finer points," Quinn reminded her. "You went right to cheating."

"Hey, I didn't have a chance against you. Cheating was the only way to ensure I'd win at least one game now and then. I was always the one paying the penalties..." Cassie's voice trailed away as she remembered the kisses she'd given as her penalty for losing.

Quinn must have remembered as well because he wasted no time in turning his attention back to Jani. "We can play a game after breakfast. How's that sound?"

Jani grinned at him. "Good. Can I have another pancake, Mama?"

Once the last pancake had been devoured, the three of them cleared off the table. Cassie insisted Jani and Quinn go play their checkers game while she did the dishes. For a few short moments she could imagine all was well in her world.

She listened as Jani chatted to Quinn in the living room where they were setting up the board. Cassie wondered if Quinn found her chatter annoying. Jani was usually a pretty quiet kid…until she got warmed up, then nothing could stop her

The game was soon underway but over pretty quickly.

"Well, Sunshine, I can't believe you beat me," Quinn said in an astonished voice.

Cassie wanted to grin at the incredulity in his voice but there was too much pain in her heart. *Sunshine.* That had been his nickname for *her.* How could he call Jani that?

A shaft of jealousy shot through Cassie for which she was immediately remorseful. How could she be jealous of her own daughter? Jani had never known her father but Cassie had had several years with him before he'd been kidnapped. She should be thrilled to see the close relationship developing between father and daughter. And she was...except for that small corner of her heart that cried out for Quinn's love and attention for herself.

It had been less than a week since he'd been released. His relationship with Renee seemed to have quickly fallen back into its old tenor in the short time they'd been together. His new relationship with Jani was good, but he hadn't shown Cassie any sign of affection or of wanting their relationship to go back to the way it had been.

"We're going for a walk, Mama."

Cassie looked down to see her daughter standing at her elbow. While she'd been lost in thought they had finished another game and she'd done up the rest of the dishes.

"Okay, sweetheart. You have fun."

"Aren't you going to come with us?" Jani asked, a furrow creasing her brow.

Cassie glanced up to where Quinn stood, not wanting to invite herself along if he preferred she didn't come. Quinn shrugged, his expression unreadable.

"Sure I'd love to come with you." Cassie decided if Quinn didn't say he didn't want her along, she was going to take advantage of the situation and go. Maybe being together more would help them get back on track.

Within minutes they were out in the crisp, pine-scented morning. Jani headed off down a path they had taken on previous visits. Quinn followed her and Cassie brought up the rear. It was a beautiful morning, and Cassie couldn't help but whispered a prayer of thanks for the beauty of God's creation and prayed for a similar beauty to unfold in her relationship with Quinn.

"See the squirrel, Mama?" Jani pointed towards a scampering brown form. Cassie stopped and watched as it hurried up a nearby tree. "I wish I could have a squirrel as a pet."

Cassie grinned. She knew exactly where this was going but before she could warn Quinn, he stepped into the trap.

"We really need to leave wild animals in the wild, Jani. They wouldn't be happy trapped in a cage."

Jani paused as if considering it. "You're right. Then maybe I could get a dog."

The trap was sprung and when only silence came from Quinn, Cassie realized he was aware of what had just happened. She decided to take pity on him and gave Jani the usual answer.

"It wouldn't be fair to get a dog, Jani. We're away from the house so much that a dog would be lonely."

Jani didn't say anything but began to march stoically down the path. Wise kid…she knew when she was defeated.

Cassie looked up at the sky. The sun danced through the overhead branches as gusts of wind moved the leaves. Suddenly Cassie found herself falling when she tripped over something lying on the path. Strong arms wrapped around her and halted her downward movement. Quinn settled her on her feet but didn't release her right away.

Cassie glanced up and suddenly was cast back in time.

"Are you all right, sunshine? Did you hurt yourself?" Quinn's brown eyes were filled with concern.

"I'm fine. You saved me!" Cassie batted her lashes. *"My hero."*

Quinn laughed. *"You probably just pretended to fall so I'd have to catch you and hold you in my arms."*

"Well, if I did, it worked." Cassie snuggled more deeply into his embrace as their lips met...

Cassie could see by Quinn's expression he too was recalling that day. She quickly stepped away from him because his expression also told her he wasn't happy about the memory.

"Sorry about that. Guess I need to keep my eyes on the path instead of the sky. Thanks for catching me." Without waiting for Quinn's response, Cassie hurried after Jani, her eyes glued to the path. She wasn't going to make the same mistake twice.

The rest of the walk passed uneventfully. Both Quinn and Cassie had little to say but thankfully Jani filled in the silence once she got over her pout about the dog.

Back at the cabin, Quinn found a couple of old fishing rods and took Jani down to the lake to cast a few lines. Cassie, who never enjoyed fishing, was only too glad to stay up at the cabin. She spent time cleaning up the inside of the cabin which sported a layer of dust after being empty for several months.

As Cassie dusted the mantel, her gaze fell on the scrapbook she and Jani had been putting together. Slowly she laid the duster down and reached for the thick book. Her fingers skimmed over the navy blue cover, her mind going back over the many hours she and Jani had spent together working on it.

Cassie sank into a nearby chair and sat staring down at the book. They had worked together on it with so many hopes and dreams of what life would be like when Quinn returned. For Jani, all those dreams seemed to be coming true but for Cassie, her dreams had shattered, leaving her feeling empty and hollow.

Against her better judgment she opened the cover, knowing the picture that would greet her. It was the one Renee had taken of her and Quinn shortly after they'd gotten engaged. Not even the sun had shone as brightly as their love for each other had that day. Looking deeply into one another's eyes, their whole future lay ahead.

Cassie closed the book and rested her arms on top of it. How long was it going to take for her to come to terms with the fact this wasn't going to be the way she'd always dreamed?

A teardrop fell onto the cover of the book and Cassie hastily brushed it away. So many tears when there should only have been smiles. When would the tears stop? When would her broken heart heal?

A noise from the front porch drew her attention. Through the screen Cassie saw Quinn and Jani climbing the steps. She brushed a quick hand over her cheeks to make sure no tears lingered. Standing she replaced the scrapbook on the mantel and turned just as they walked into the cabin.

They paused on the mat inside the door, both of them soaking wet.

"What on earth happened?" Cassie asked as she hurried to Jani's side.

Jani stared at the floor and offered no explanation so Cassie looked at Quinn.

"She was standing too near the edge of the dock and when she thought she got a bite she got a little excited and sort of slipped into the water. I went in after her."

"Well, I'm glad no one was hurt," Cassie said, rubbing her hand over Jani's back. "Why don't you get out of those wet clothes and I'll stick them in the washer."

Quinn nodded and headed for the stairs while Cassie steered Jani in the direction of the bathroom. Jani was uncharacteristically quiet as Cassie got her undressed and into the shower. She kept her gaze averted and uttered not a word of complaint when Cassie said she'd have to wash her hair.

"Jani, sweetheart, what's wrong? Did you get hurt when you fell?"

Jani shook her head no but didn't say a word.

Cassie cupped her daughter's chin and forced her to meet her gaze. Misery clouded her normally clear, sparkling eyes.

"Oh sweetheart, what's wrong?" Cassie asked again.

"Is Daddy mad at me?" Jani asked, her voice tremulous. "For falling into the water and making him get all wet?

Cassie shook her head. "No, darling, he's not."

Some of the misery began to fade. "Are you sure?"

"I'm sure. I think you probably scared him when you fell in, but he's not mad."

Jani seemed to relax and the tension ebbed from her face. "I almost caught a great big fish."

"Did you really?" Cassie asked, amazed at the resiliency of youth.

Jani was pretty much back to her old self by the time they left the bathroom, her small body swaddled in a towel.

"You go on and get changed while I put your clothes in the washer."

Jani disappeared into the bedroom as Cassie gathered the wet clothes from the bathroom floor. When she came back out of the bathroom Quinn stood there, holding his own bundle of wet clothes.

Chapter Five

"Well, it looks like the two of you survived your dunking no worse for wear," Cassie commented with a smile.

"It was certainly colder than I had anticipated, but I'm used to bathing in cold water so it wasn't too much of a shock."

"Jani thought maybe you were mad at her because of what happened." Cassie cocked her head to the side. "I assured her you weren't."

"No, I wasn't, although she probably scared a good ten years off my life."

"I guess I should have told you that Jani does know how to swim. I knew we couldn't spend any length of time up here with her being so near the water if she didn't know how. She learned at an early age. But thanks for jumping in after her."

"I'd hardly have left her in there to fend for herself," Quinn said defensively. "I may not know much about being a father, but I do know that when your child is in a dangerous situation you try your best to rescue them."

Cassie fumbled for the words to reply. "I, uh, didn't mean to imply that you wouldn't have rescued her. I am truly grateful you went in after her. She is my world. If anything happened to her..."

Agony clenched Cassie's heart at the thought. Jani had been the one thing that had kept her sane all these years and it looked like she would be the only physical link Cassie had to the wonderful, happy time she and Quinn had shared together before the kidnapping. Cassie couldn't imagine losing her.

Struggling to keep her emotions under control, Cassie held out her hand. "I'll put your clothes into the washer with Jani's."

Quinn handed them over without comment and Cassie left him standing in the living room while she went to the small room that served as storage and laundry room. With trembling hands she pushed the clothes into the washer and added the detergent before switching it on.

After the machine started, Cassie stood there, her hands braced on the vibrating machine for a few moments, trying to gather herself back together. Too many emotions were bubbling near the surface. She didn't want them to spill over in front of Quinn or Jani. They needed to be kept for times of privacy and solitude.

When she returned to the living room Jani stood there, dressed and trying to dry her hair. Cassie grabbed a comb from the bathroom and sat down on a chair, pulling Jani to stand between her legs. As Cassie worked the comb through the long strands of wet hair she listened to Jani tell Quinn about her other attempts at both fishing and swimming in the lake.

Out of the corner of her eye Cassie watched Quinn, glad to see Jani had lost her fear of his being angry with her.

It didn't sink in right away but suddenly she realized he wore the same shirt he'd worn the day before.

"We need to go shopping," Cassie blurted out before she could catch herself. Both Jani and Quinn looked at her. "Sorry, I just realized you probably need more clothes, Quinn. We can go to town later and pick you up a few more things."

"That's not necessary," Quinn objected. "I'm fine with what I have."

"But you only have a couple of pairs of jeans and shirts. You need more than that."

"I'll get some when we get back to the city and I get my hands on some money."

"You don't need to worry about that, I have money," Cassie told him. When she saw his expression darken she knew she'd said the wrong thing.

"I won't take your money. You've worked hard for it." Quinn replied, his voice hard and unyielding.

"It's not my money, Quinn," Cassie said softly. "It's our money. We're a family."

Quinn remained silent. To Cassie, his words had been like yet another nail in the coffin of her dreams. He wouldn't even take her money. He wouldn't take anything from her. He wanted nothing she had to offer. Except her daughter.

Cassie looked away and stared into the fireplace that lay as empty and dark as her future.

"Consider it a loan," Cassie said flatly. "The inheritance from your dad is waiting for you. You can pay me back when you get money from your account. You need more clothes."

"Fine. I'll pay you for whatever I spend," Quinn agreed although Cassie could hear the reluctance in his voice.

"If we want to get to the stores before they close we'd better leave soon."

Within short order, Cassie sat behind the wheel of the SUV headed for the closest town with a small shopping center. She had not anticipated things getting worse once they were at the mall but they did.

The young salesgirl in charge of the men's section seemed only too willing to help Quinn out. She ignored Cassie and Jani and focused her attention on Quinn, doing her best to keep his attention on her.

Cassie looked at Quinn more closely and realized she had only recognized the differences from the way he'd been before. She had not realized how attractive this new ruggedness was. His darkened skin and lean, muscular body suddenly captured her attention as it had the salesgirl's.

Startled, Cassie caught herself, guilt flooding her. It felt wrong to admire the way Quinn looked now. Almost as if she was betraying the Quinn she'd married. Confused, Cassie looked away from where he stood selecting jeans.

Jealousy and confusion ate away at her. She'd never before felt jealousy where Quinn was concerned with other women. He'd always made her feel secure in his love and affection. And he'd had no trouble letting the world know he was committed to her.

Cassie's gaze went to Quinn's left hand. His bare left hand. Even the ring she'd chosen for him was gone. Did any part of the old Quinn remain?

"I think I have enough for now," Quinn said, interrupting her thoughts.

Cassie nodded and followed him to the cash register to pay for his purchases. She breathed a sigh of relief when they left the store and escaped the salesgirl's flirtatiousness.

"Do you want to get something to eat before we head back to the cabin?" she asked as they walked towards the doors of the mall. "There are a couple of burger places and a pizza parlor close by."

"Pizza," Jani and Quinn replied in unison. They grinned at each other.

"Pizza it is."

From the look of the empty, dirty tables in the nearby pizza parlor they'd just missed the dinnertime rush. The hostess apologized for the wait and told them a table would be cleared for them in a few minutes. The tantalizing aroma of tomatoes and cheese hung in the air and Cassie realized just how hungry she was.

Once seated at their table Quinn left the ordering up to Cassie.

"Anything you order is fine with me," he told her. "I'm not too particular about what I eat as long as it's not rice or beans."

"I want a cheese one, Mama," Jani piped up. "Nothing else on it."

Cassie nodded. "I remember, sweetheart."

The waitress returned and Cassie placed their order.

Silence descended on their table once the waitress had left. Even Jani was quiet for a change. She busily looked at all the old movie pictures on the wall next to their booth.

Thankfully the silence wasn't too noticeable since the conversation from the few nearby occupied tables was loud enough to cover it. But to Cassie it was deafening since there would never have been that kind of silence with the old Quinn. They always had something to talk about.

"Cassie!"

Hearing her name, Cassie turned and saw an older woman approaching their table.

"Hi, Muriel," she said, hoping her dismay didn't show.

Cassie hadn't really wanted to run into anyone who knew her but that was unrealistic since her family had been vacationing in the area all of her life.

"Honey, you didn't let us know you were coming up here." Muriel's gaze moved to Quinn. "Quinn, it's great to see you again. We heard the news on the radio."

"It's good to be back," Quinn replied with a nod of his head.

"Will you be in church tomorrow?" Muriel asked.

Cassie wasn't sure about Quinn but she planned to go with Jani. "We'll be there."

"Great. We'll see you then."

Cassie sighed with relief as the woman moved away. She was glad Muriel hadn't made a big fuss out of Quinn's presence. Many people had prayed over the years for Quinn and Cassie hated to be so selfish about sharing him, but she herself hadn't really gotten to know the new man her husband had become.

"Can I go play one of the games, Mom?" Jani asked, pointing to the corner of the room where several arcade games stood. "I want to play the bopping one."

Cassie pulled out her wallet and slide four quarters towards Jani. "When those are gone, that's it, okay?"

Jani nodded, her ponytail bouncing with the movement. "Want to come, Daddy?"

Quinn slid out of the booth and followed Jani towards the games. Cassie turned in her seat to watch them. Seeing them together filled her heart with joy. It was the one area of the reunion where her emotions weren't mixed. This new Quinn was a great dad, as good a dad as the old Quinn might have been. That he loved Jani was obvious and the little girl clearly returned his feelings. Cassie was happy for both of them. She just wished she didn't feel like the proverbial third wheel. It seemed to her Quinn tolerated her presence simply because of Jani, that if there had been no Jani, they wouldn't be together now.

"Looks like they're having fun," a voice interrupted Cassie's thoughts.

Cassie looked around to see the waitress slipping the pizza and pop onto the table. "Yes, my daughter really likes that game. But she likes pizza more so I imagine she'll be back pretty quick."

The waitress smiled as she watched Jani look over, spot the pizza and immediately abandoned the game. "Looks like you're right."

"Oh yum," Jani exclaimed as she slid into the booth just as the waitress left.

Quinn sat down next to her but didn't seem to be eyeing the pizza with as much excitement.

"Are you okay?" Cassie asked him.

"I'm fine." Quinn replied, still staring at the pizza. "I just keep forgetting that loading my system with this kind of food doesn't sit real well. I guess my digestive system is still set for beans and rice."

"Does it even bother you if you eat small amounts?"

"Not as much but when I'm hungry, small amounts don't always fill me up."

"We can buy some rice if you'd like. Maybe gradually decreasing your rice and increasing other foods would work better than changing so quickly."

Quinn shrugged. "Probably but to be perfectly honest, I never want to eat another bite of rice in my life."

Cassie fell silent. It seemed nothing she tried to do for Quinn was what he wanted. In silence she picked up her piece of pizza and took a bite. Quinn also took a slice and began to eat it, apparently willing to risk feeling sick later.

"Another piece, please, Mama," Jani requested after she'd polished off her first.

Cassie gave her a slice and took another slice for herself. Quinn also took a second slice once he finished his first. Between the three of them they managed to finish off all but one piece of the pizza. Cassie had the waitress wrap it up knowing Jani would gladly eat it the next day.

Once back at the cabin, Cassie helped Jani get ready for bed. They read a story together and then went looking for Quinn to join them while Jani said her prayers. They couldn't find him in the house so Cassie assumed he had gone out to the water.

"Where's Daddy?" Jani asked, a concerned look on her small face. "He's not gone again, is he? I never want him to be gone again."

Cassie tucked Jani's blanket in around her and sat down on the edge of the bed. "He's not gone. I think he's probably down by the dock. Why don't we say your prayers together and then I'll go find him to come kiss you goodnight?"

Jani nodded and closed her eyes. "Dear Jesus, thank you for bringing Daddy home. We missed him so much. Help him to be happy."

Cassie's eyes popped open and she stared at her daughter's face. Jani's eyes were tightly closed, her expression earnest. It amazed—and dismayed—Cassie that Jani had picked up on Quinn's unhappiness. How she wished she could protect her daughter from further hurt.

Closing her eyes again, Cassie asked God why things had ended up this way. Why had He allowed Quinn to return to them in this condition? What should have been the happiest time in their lives was turning into the worst. It just wasn't fair.

"Mommy, I said amen," Jani said as she pulled on Cassie's sleeve to get her attention.

"Sorry, Baby, Mama was just saying a little prayer of her own."

"Will you go find Daddy now?"

Cassie nodded and bent to press a kiss to Jani's soft cheek. "I'll go get him."

*****

Quinn stood at the end of the dock. A soft breeze blew across the water causing goose bumps to pop up on his arms. He slipped his hands into the pockets of his jeans and stared out at the lake. During the first couple years he'd been a hostage, he'd dreamed of nights like this. He'd dreamed of Cassie joining him on the dock. Of sitting together, their feet dangling in the icy water below the dock. Of sharing dreams and hopes for their future. Of their life together. Now there was no desire in Quinn to do that. It had all been killed inside him. Nothing remained of him but an empty shell. The only emotions within his soul were ugly and dark.

Well, not all, he reminded himself. The one bright spot, the only bright spot was Jani. If it hadn't been for her he would have left as soon as he had let Cassie know he was still alive. Left her to get on with her life without him. Because he knew she'd be much better off. Why couldn't she just see that and make things easier on all of them? He was broken…an empty shell of the man she'd fallen in love with.

"Quinn?" For a moment, Quinn thought he imagined the soft sound of Cassie's voice like he had years ago but then quickly realized she stood behind him.

He turned but couldn't see her clearly as the trees cast shadows over her. Even without seeing Cassie he could sense the tension in her. He had always been able to sense stuff like that about her, but never before had the tension been directed at him.

"Jani wants to say good night to you," Cassie said softly.

Quinn nodded and headed off the dock. He thought Cassie might fall into step beside him, but when he glanced over his shoulder he saw her standing at the water's edge, her back to him. It was such a familiar scene, Cassie had always been drawn to the water when she was troubled, and yet so strange. He couldn't believe how far apart two people could become when they had once been so close.

Turning his thoughts from Cassie he went into the house to see his daughter. Jani lay on her side watching the doorway, waiting for him.

"Good night, sweetheart," Quinn said as he bent to kiss her.

"Night, Daddy." Jani's voice was soft and drowsy. "I love you."

The words clenched Quinn's heart. He hadn't heard them in so long. "I love you, too, Jani."

He crouched down next to the bed and gently stroked her hair, watching as her eyelids slowly closed and her breathing deepened. He stayed for a few more minutes looking at the daughter he and Cassie had created out of their love. He wished he could find that love again, but it just seemed to be gone.

When Quinn finally left Jani's side he found Cassie in the kitchen. His first instinct was to climb the stairs to the loft and avoid her. He found it difficult to look at her and see the pain and heartache in her eyes. It was even harder to know that he put it there and didn't know how to take it away. He didn't think he'd be doing either of them any favors by pretending something he didn't feel.

Cassie turned around just then and saw him standing in the living room. "Do you want something to drink before bed?"

Quinn walked to the kitchen and pulled out a chair at the table. "I wouldn't mind a cup of hot chocolate, if you have some."

"We always have hot chocolate," Cassie reminded him.

As she began to prepare the hot chocolate Quinn looked at her, really looked at her and for the first time clearly saw the differences in her. Oh, there were physical ones that were obvious. She'd cut her hair a bit and put on a few pounds, both of which looked good on her. She was still a very attractive woman, Quinn acknowledged to himself, but for some reason it just didn't stir his heart the way it once had.

"Here you go." Cassie placed a mug in front of him on the table. She got another cup from the counter and sat down across from him. Her slender fingers wrapped around the mug as she lifted it to her lips and took a sip. "I know this might not be the time to get into a discussion, but I think we need to talk."

Quinn sighed. No, it wasn't the time, but then as far as he was concerned, he'd rather not ever have the discussion Cassie wanted. Unfortunately, he knew he owed her that much. They couldn't live in limbo forever.

"Yes, we need to talk." Quinn took a sip of his chocolate and put the mug back on the table. "Now is as good a time as any."

Cassie looked at him in surprise "Now? Are you sure?"

Quinn shrugged. "We need to talk and Jani's asleep so I think it's a good time."

"Of course, you're right. It is important we do this when Jani's not around."

An awkward silence grew between them as Quinn waited for Cassie to go first.

"What was it like?"

Her question surprised Quinn. It wasn't the one he had imagined she'd ask first. "Being hostage? Why?"

Cassie shrugged. "Maybe knowing more about what you went through will help me to understand the person you are now."

Quinn really doubted that would happen. Understanding could only come through experiencing it and he didn't wish that on Cassie. Still, if she wanted to know, he would tell her.

"It was physically rough at first. We kept on the move a lot through the wet rain forest. The bugs drove me nuts and I would constantly be slapping at them but after a while I toughened up physically and learned to ignore them the way the others did. I was never given much to eat. But then, they didn't have a lot so I guess

I was fortunate to get what I did. Lots of rice and beans. Sometimes we'd have a bit of meat. It wasn't fancy, that's for sure.

"They kept me confined in a cage like structure for the last few years after we finally stopped moving around so much. Before that, I was tied at all times and someone was always with me."

Quinn stopped to reflect on what he'd told Cassie. He knew she must have been wondering how that could have changed him so much. He'd told her the easy part, but he wasn't sure he could tell her the rest. How could he put into words the agonizing mental torture he'd gone through? How could he explain to her how it was to never be alone and yet feel gut-wrenching loneliness?

Gazing down at the hot chocolate in the mug Quinn was reminded of some of the rivers they'd crossed that had looked similar to the brown liquid in his cup. He'd lost count of how many times they slogged through water trying to put more and more distance between them and whoever followed them. At times he'd wondered if anyone was actually following them. Were they out searching for him? Or had the thought of trying to pierce the canopy of forest to find him been too overwhelming for the searchers?

Quinn glanced up and saw Cassie watching him, her gaze reserved. How could he make her understand the loneliness that took over once the initial fear had faded? Within a day of being captured, the four missionaries had been separated and Quinn never saw any of the other men again. None of his captors spoke English and his Spanish was too basic at that point for holding any type of in-depth conversation.

He had missed Cassie fiercely and worried about what his kidnapping was doing to her. As time passed with no sign of release in sight, Quinn had begun to fear his life would end at any moment. He hadn't wanted to die. Even though he knew he was going to heaven, he'd wanted to see Cassie just one more time. He had held hour-long talks with God, pleading for release. Pleading for a chance to see Cassie again. Sometimes he'd sing hymns and choruses from church or recite the verses he'd memorized.

That had gotten him through the first year but the constant fear and loneliness began to wear on him mentally so he'd begun to shut it out. He began to turn it off and his talks with God became shorter and less frequent. The music left his soul. By the end of the second year he'd succeeded in walling off any emotions and with each successive year that wall had only gotten thicker and more impenetrable, especially with the arrival of that final leader. He had succeeded in driving the last of Quinn's emotions deep down within him.

Realizing Cassie was still waiting for him to continue, Quinn cleared his throat and tried to gather his thoughts. "I'm sure you heard from David that we were separated after that first day. It was difficult being with a group of men who basically held my life in their hands and yet I had no way of communicating with them. For all I knew, they were sitting around the fire at night discussing how they were going to kill me the next day.

"At first the days seemed long and endless but eventually they began to blur into one another and there were times I didn't even know what day of the week it was. And frankly, I didn't care. One day was pretty much the same as the other."

"Did you ever try to escape?" Cassie asked.

Quinn took another sip of his cocoa then shook his head. "I thought about it a lot. When you're held captive I think it's only natural you think about it, but I knew that even if I did get away, I probably wouldn't get very far. We stayed in the jungle most of the time with no discernible trails. Knowing my luck I would have walked in a circle and ended up right back at the camp. I figured it would be easier to die of a gunshot than of starvation in the jungle."

"Were there..." Cassie began then paused, chewing on her lower lip.

"Were there what?" Quinn prompted her.

"Women. Were there women?" Cassie asked, the words coming in a rush.

"As part of the kidnappers who took us initially? No. There were a few women in the group once we started moving. They were the wives of some of the men and took care of the cooking. For the last year or so we were pretty much in the same place so there were more women around. Kids, too. We were in a small encampment buried deep in the jungle somewhere."

Quinn saw Cassie chew her lip again, as if she hadn't asked her real question. Finally her gaze met his.

"I meant was there a woman...a woman for you."

Chapter Six

Cassie gripped her mug tightly. She wasn't sure where the question had come from but it had been a thought lingering in the back of her mind for a day or so now.

Quinn scowled. "You mean like a mistress or something?"

"Yes." Cassie hoped he couldn't hear the quivering in her voice. "I know that sometimes in situations like yours it happens."

"Well, that may have happened with others but it didn't with me. Why would you even think that?"

Cassie shrugged. "You've been so distant since you came home. It's pretty clear the feelings you once had for me are gone. I thought maybe it was because someone else had captured your heart, as well as your body."

"I would have thought you'd know me better than to suspect something like that. I would never do that to you."

"The Quinn I married would never have done it to me." Cassie ran her fingers along the smooth sides of the mug. "Everything I've seen since you got back tells me you are no longer that man. In fact, it feels as if you've gone out of your way to prove to me you aren't that Quinn. It's clear you lost your faith while you were out in that jungle, I just didn't know what else you might have lost."

Quinn just stared at her, his expression hard. It seemed as if he was trying to come up with something to refute her logic but couldn't.

"I would never have betrayed our marriage vows. Did I have the opportunity? Well, since you asked, yes, I did, but I never once took advantage of it. I wasn't even tempted. I may have lost my faith but my morals are still intact."

Cassie stood and took her mug to the sink. She turned on the water, ran some into the mug and swished it around before turning it upside down in the sink.

"I'd like to go back to the city tomorrow." Quinn said.

"So soon?" she asked.

"I want to see my mom. And I just think it would be…easier in the city."

Cassie stared out the window over the sink into the darkness beyond. She wasn't sure how she felt about heading home. It certainly wasn't the way she'd envisioned leaving the cabin. She'd been so sure they'd be returning home as a family with their future bright ahead of them. This fractured relationship was not what she wanted to take back to her home.

She heard the scrap of a chair and glanced back to see Quinn standing near the table.

"We can leave after lunch if you'd like," Quinn said.

Cassie watched him turn to leave and then hesitate. He slowly turned back towards her.

"One more thing. I don't want to hurt you more than I already have but..." He cleared his throat. "I need some space. I'm going to stay with Renee for a while."

Cassie jerked back to face the window, her hands gripping the edge of the sink. She heard Quinn's footsteps leave the kitchen and was glad he hadn't waited for her to respond. Once alone, Cassie bent forward trying to contain the pain spreading through her midsection. His announcement had been a kick to her gut.

Steeling herself against the pain, Cassie straightened and methodically finished washing their mugs. She dried them off and put them back into the cupboard. Slowly she began to prepare the kitchen for their departure the next day. Two weeks had been shortened into two days…

How much more was she going to be asked to bear?

Cassie scrubbed the counter with more force than necessary. *How come this is happening to me, God? How come you brought him home to me only to have him reject our marriage?*

"Why are you doing this to me?" She forced the question through the tight muscles of her throat.

Cassie continued her questioning of God while she finished up in the kitchen. She headed for the bedroom to pack her stuff but detoured as she walked through the living room and headed out the front door.

Slow measured steps took her across the rough wood porch to the stairs onto the grass below. Without even thinking of her destination, Cassie automatically headed for her rock. The evening cool tried to pierce the thickness of her sweater, but Cassie ignored it. Just as she tried to ignore the coldness that had invaded her body, starting with her heart.

On the rock Cassie sat down and pulled her legs up to rest her chin on her knees. She gazed out across the water. In the past its serenity would have eased her tension but tonight a wind blew across the lake causing the water to ripple and become choppy. Just like her life.

Why, God? The question repeated itself in an endless loop in her mind. *Why?*

I am God. The words from a verse came to mind, interrupting the question briefly.

"I know You are God," Cassie whispered, her words floating away on the breeze from the lake. "But why?"

Be still.

"Be still," Cassie repeated. She was far from still. Her emotions were running rampant, her mind constantly seeking answers. Being still just wasn't on the agenda.

"Cass?" Quinn's voice jerked her out of her frozen state.

She didn't watch him as he climbed onto the rock and sat next to her. In the past they'd sat together on the rock but never so close without touching. Never so close and yet so far apart.

"I'm sorry if my decision has hurt you. I didn't want to but right now I just need some space. I need some time to figure myself out without trying to figure our marriage out."

"What's to figure out, Quinn? We're married. We have a daughter who needs us. What are you going to tell her? She expects you to live with us."

Quinn sat silently for a few long moments before responding. "I know. I'll tell her in the morning. Somehow I'll help her understand this is best for now."

Cassie felt tears well up. "How is she going to understand when I don't?"

There was no response to her question but then Cassie hadn't really expected one. Something told her Quinn was as confused by all of this as she was. That was why he wanted space. Part of her understood but she didn't think it was necessary to stay apart. Cassie was so afraid that if Quinn didn't come home now, he never would.

They sat together for a while longer but the silence was uncomfortable and soon Cassie couldn't stand it. "Maybe I should leave Jani home from church with you so that you can explain it to her."

"Okay, I'll talk to her while you're gone."

Cassie stood up and jumped off the rock to the ground below. "I'm going to bed. See you in the morning."

Without waiting for Quinn to respond Cassie headed for the house and the sleepless night she was sure lay ahead.

*****

Quinn watched Cassie walk away, her slender figure moving slowly in and out of the dappled shadows of the trees. Finally she disappeared into the cabin and Quinn turned back to the lake.

For the first time since returning, Quinn felt a pang of pain. A crack in the wall guarding his emotions. His head dipped. Why couldn't he have just died out there in that jungle? He was causing nothing but pain with his return. His marriage was a mess because he just couldn't find the feelings he'd once had in order to get it back into shape. And more than that, the future they'd once planned had been founded on their faith, a faith they had shared. A faith he no longer had.

Jani was his only bright spot, the only weakness he allowed in his emotions. But even with her there was still a part of him that was buried deep. The man who would have cried at the birth of his daughter was not there anymore. Those deep, overwhelming emotions were gone now. Jani seemed to accept him, why couldn't Cassie?

*****

Cassie rose to bright sunshine the next morning. She wished her mood was even half as bright. She was in the kitchen making French toast for breakfast when Jani woke up.

"Mornin', Mama," Jani sang out as she danced into the kitchen. She looked so adorable with her slightly mussed hair and flushed cheeks. How Cassie wished she could protect her from what lay ahead.

"Morning, sweetheart." Cassie bent and pressed a kiss to her soft cheek. "Want some French toast?"

Jani nodded as she slid onto a chair at the table. "And chocolate milk?"

"Sure." Cassie busied herself getting Jani's breakfast ready.

"Is today church, Mama?" Jani asked when Cassie set the plate in front of her.

"Let's pray for your food first then I'll talk to you about church, okay?"

Once the prayer was said and Jani started eating, Cassie tried to explain what the day held. "Daddy isn't going to church this morning. He'd rather not be around a lot of people yet. I'm going to go to church but Daddy wants you to stay with him so you can spend some time together and talk. Is that okay?"

With her mouth full of French toast, Jani just nodded. Before she could say anything more Quinn joined them and sat down at the table with Jani.

"Hey, Sunshine. How are you this morning?" Quinn asked Jani.

Cassie turned away from the two of them, the pain piercing her again at the sound of Quinn calling Jani by the name he used to call her. Would it ever get easier?

She loaded up a plate for Quinn and set it in front of him. "I've already told Jani she'll be staying home with you today. I'll finish getting stuff together to leave after church."

Quinn nodded and began to eat. Cassie hadn't bothered to sample any of the breakfast she'd prepared. The hollow in her stomach made it impossible to eat anything without feeling as if she would throw up.

She left Jani and Quinn eating their breakfast and went to change. As Cassie slipped the simple blue sheath dress over her head she struggled to not dwell on how this was one more thing that wasn't going according to plan. She knew it was time to chuck the plan. It was the only way to keep from bursting into tears every time something didn't go as she had hoped.

Cassie stood in front of the mirror and stared at herself. What did Quinn see when he looked her? Did he see the shorter hair instead of the long he had loved? Did he see the extra pounds her pregnancy had added to her frame?

With a fingertip Cassie touched the corner of her eye. She had a few more tiny wrinkles than she had had six years ago. Life had not been all that kind to her. Sighing, Cassie began to look through her makeup bag for the items that would hopefully hide the wrinkles and the dark circles beneath her eyes.

Twenty minutes later she was ready to go. Quinn and Jani were in the kitchen at the sink doing dishes. Cassie stood for a moment watching them. This was something she had imagined and hoped would be. Father and daughter. Together.

"I'm going now." Cassie said, interrupting their laughter.

Jani dried her hands on the towel Quinn held and jumped off the small stool. Cassie gave her a hug and kissed the top of her head. She wondered if the joy would be gone from Jani's eyes when she returned.

For a moment Cassie toyed with the idea of staying. She was so used to being there for Jani. Protecting her from pain, easing the hurts, both physical and emotional. Her instinct was to stay. Her baby's dreams for their family were going to be crushed right along with her mother's.

She looked at Quinn and found him watching her, the dishtowel still in his hands. He was Jani's father. Cassie had to trust him to protect her as well.

"I'll be back in a while." Cassie gave Jani one more quick hug and released her. She grabbed her Bible and purse and with one last look at the two people she loved most in the world, Cassie left the cabin.

She tried not to think about Quinn and Jani as she guided the car along the winding road to the small town where the church was. It dawned on her as she approached the small building that there would be questions about why she was alone.

She couldn't avoid it though as one of the church members spotted her and waved. Having attended the church every time her family had been at the cabin, most members knew Cassie well.

She parked the SUV and gathered up her stuff. The pastor stood on the steps greeting people as they entered. "Where's that adorable daughter of yours? And your husband? We were looking forward to seeing him again after all these years of praying for his release."

The hollow in Cassie's stomach grew. She took a deep breath and for the first time in her life, told a half-truth to a pastor. "He's not feeling up to being around a lot of people just yet. And Jani's not ready to let her daddy out of her sight for very long so I let her stay with him."

The pastor nodded, understanding in his warm brown eyes. "Maybe next week."

"Actually, we're heading back to the city this afternoon. Quinn needs to spend some time with the rest of his family."

"I'm sorry to hear you're leaving so soon. Hopefully you'll be back out in the next few months so we can see Quinn."

"I hope so." Cassie stretched the muscles of her face into what she hoped was a smile even though it felt more like a grimace. "You know how we like it out here."

Cassie moved past the pastor into the church, stopping frequently to repeat the story she'd first told on the steps of the small church. Would it ever end? Maybe it would have been better if she'd skipped church too. Her heart was just not into worshipping the Lord. In fact, there was a small part of her heart that was very angry with Him right then.

How could He allow her family to fall apart after all they'd been through? All they'd suffered because they had been following His call to be missionaries?

Sitting in a pew near the back Cassie struggled to get her heart into the right attitude for worship. She couldn't even sing the choruses. It seemed so hypocritical to sing songs of praise and thanksgiving when her heart just wasn't in it. Cassie's hands clenched the pew in front of her as they stood to pray.

Anguish gripped her heart as she listened to the pastor thank God for Quinn's safe arrival and for the reuniting of their family. Tears threatened to flow but she wouldn't let them escape. No one here would understand why she shed tears when she should be happy.

Cassie tuned out the sounds around her and struggled to maintain control. She shouldn't be there. The temptation to grab her Bible and leave was great but Cassie didn't want to draw even more attention to herself so she went through the motions of worship, sitting when the congregation sat, standing when they did.

When the pastor finally stood to give his message Cassie thought her head was going to explode from the tension filling her. She rubbed her temples trying to ease the ache.

Normally the pastor's sermons were uplifting and Cassie went away from the service feeling encouraged and hopeful. Today it took all her strength to just keep her gaze forward so at least it looked like she was paying attention. Unfortunately, she didn't want to hear a sermon about prayer. Her prayers apparently didn't work too well. God had only answered half of her prayer for Quinn to come home and not for their family to be reunited. She didn't want to think about why God would allow their family to fall apart, why He wouldn't answer her prayer.

Cassie was the first one out the door when the service ended. She said a quick goodbye to the pastor who once again stood at the doorway, promising to bring Quinn the next time they came to the cabin.

Even though she didn't feel very hungry Cassie stopped at a takeout restaurant and bought a bucket of chicken before heading back to Quinn and Jani.

The cabin was quiet when she arrived. Cassie set her Bible and the chicken on the table and went to the kitchen. From the small window she could see Quinn and Jani sitting on the rock. Had Quinn told Jani yet? Cassie hoped so. She didn't know how she would react if she had to be a part of that conversation.

Cassie watched as they sat close together talking and pointing at things out over the water. Theirs was a relationship that would not falter. Father and daughter. It was what Cassie had always hoped to see but somehow she'd been a part of that picture too, in her dreams. It hurt to be on the outside looking in.

Slowly Cassie turned from the window and began to get stuff ready for lunch. She had just set the chicken out when she heard steps on the front porch and looked up to see Jani and Quinn enter the house.

"Mama!" Jani smiled when she saw her and ran to give her a hug.

As Cassie embraced her daughter she looked at Quinn hoping he could read the question in her eyes. He gave a brief nod but his expression didn't change. Cassie wanted to ask Jani about it but instead took her daughter's small face in her hands and tilted it up for a kiss.

"Want some chicken? I stopped for it on my way home."

"Yum!" Jani scrambled onto her chair and leaned forward onto the table to smell it. "My favorite!"

In between bites, Jani chatted excitedly about the walk they had taken that morning. Her appetite all but gone, Cassie picked at her chicken waiting to hear her daughter say something about the news Quinn had given her. Instead it seemed she touched on every topic but that.

After they finished Cassie sent Jani to her room to finish packing up her things. When the little girl was out of earshot she leaned towards Quinn. "You did talk to her, right?"

Quinn nodded. "I told her I'd be staying with Aunt Renee when we got back."

"What did she say to that?"

"It didn't seem to faze her. She just asked if she could come over whenever she wanted to see me. I told her she could."

Cassie's heart sank. With Jani taking it this well there was no need for Quinn to even consider staying together as a family. Hoping the agony she felt in her heart wasn't evident on her face, Cassie stood and began to clear the table.

"I'll go start loading up the vehicle," Quinn said as he stood.

"Mama, I've got everything in my bag," Jani said, coming out of the small bedroom.

"Okay, sweetie. Give it to Daddy and he'll put it in the car."

In less than an hour the cabin was locked up and they were on their way back to the city. Cassie looked in her rearview mirror as they drove away and wondered if they would ever again create happy memories in the cabin. They rounded a corner and the cabin disappeared from her view, shrouded by trees. It seemed as if a door had just slammed shut on all the hopes and dreams she'd had. Cassie had no idea what lay ahead. All she knew was that she was very afraid.

Chapter Seven

"Do you want me to take you straight to Renee's?" Cassie asked as they neared the outskirts of the city.

"I think that would be best," Quinn said quietly.

The whole trip had been strained. Even Jani had given up chattering and fallen asleep. What was one supposed to say to a man who was her husband but didn't want to be, Cassie wondered. It seemed there were no words appropriate for that.

It wasn't long before they pulled up in front of Renee's house. Renee was clearly surprised when she opened the door and saw them standing there.

"Hey! What are you guys doing back? I thought you were out at the cabin for a couple of weeks?" Renee stepped back and waved with her hand. "Come on in."

"Hi, Sis," Quinn said and leaned down to kiss her cheek.

Cassie could feel Renee's gaze on her. She quickly bent to say something to Jani, fearing she'd burst into tears if she saw the questions in Renee's eyes.

"How's my little princess?" Renee asked as she gave Jani a hug.

When Cassie approached, Renee embraced her tightly. "What's up, Cass?" she asked softly in her ear.

Cassie kept her gaze down as Renee pulled back and looked at her. "You'll have to ask your brother." Tears were so near the surface. "I need to use your bathroom."

Renee released Cassie's arms and nodded.

Cassie escaped down the hallway and, ignoring the bathroom on the first floor, went up the stairs to the small one off Renee's bedroom. Once inside she leaned back against the door, her breath coming in gulping sobs.

*****

Quinn didn't much care for the look on Renee's face. He'd seen that determined look before and it never boded well for him.

"Okay, now that Jani's settled watching her video why don't you tell me what's going on," Renee suggested as she sat in the chair across from Quinn. "You were supposed to be up at the cabin for a couple of weeks at least and yet here you are and it's not even been a week. Not to mention the fact that Cassie looks awful. What happened?"

How could he explain to her, Quinn wondered, what it was like to be dropped into a situation where everyone expected him to act one way because of who they thought he was?

"I'm waiting," Renee reminded him, her fingernails tapping rhythmically on the arm of the chair she sat in.

If it had been possible to get away without having to explain to her, Quinn would have done it but he needed her. More precisely, he needed somewhere to stay and hers was the cheapest place around.

"Things aren't working out how Cassie had hoped."

"How *Cassie* had hoped?" Renee asked, stressing Cassie's name. "I would have thought you had the same hopes. You've just come home after being held captive for several years and it's not your hope to reunite your family too?"

Quinn sighed. "It's more difficult than that, Renee. I've changed a lot in the years I was held hostage. I'm not the person Cassie fell in love with. I'm not the person she built her dreams for her future around."

Renee leaned back in her chair, her eyes narrowed as she looked at him. "It's not like her dreams are that unreasonable, Quinn. She hoped that you'd be released and that you'd be together as a family again. I guess I don't see the problem."

"I don't think I'd make a good husband to Cassie right now. I lost a lot of things out there in the jungle and not all of them were material." Quinn rubbed his left hand where his wedding ring had once been. "I lost my faith in God. I lost the joy of living. I lost...love."

"Are you telling me you don't love Cassie anymore?" Renee asked, sadness in her eyes. "I didn't think that would ever happen. Your love for each other was rare and beautiful. It was something I looked for in every relationship I had. And never seemed to find. I can't believe that love is just gone." Suddenly her expression hardened. "You haven't tried hard enough. You need to go to counseling or something."

"Renee, for now I need a place to stay. What happens after that I don't know."

Quinn saw the set of Renee's jaw and wondered if she would actually refuse to let him stay with her. He sensed the war within her, her loyalty to Cassie as a friend versus her loyalty to him as her brother.

Renee stood and began to pace. "What about Jani? Have you told her about your decision to not live with them?"

Quinn nodded. "I talked to her earlier today. She took it really well."

"What did you tell her? Did you make promises you don't intend to keep?" Renee demanded.

"No. I told her that her mommy and I couldn't live together right now but that we still loved her. She said she had a friend like that and that she had lots of toys since she had two bedrooms. Jani wanted to know if she could still see me whenever she wanted. I told her yes."

Renee shook her head. "Life seems so simple when you're a child. And it's a sad state of the world when a child is so accepting of her parents not living together because she has friends that live a life like that. It should be the exception, not the norm."

Quinn had to agree. He'd never thought he'd be half of a separated couple. *But you don't have to be.* The thought popped into his mind but Quinn pushed it away. He didn't want to consider that option. It was just too hard for him and for Cassie.

"Okay, so you want a place to stay. How long are you going to need it?" Renee settled back into her chair.

Quinn shrugged. "I don't know. I'm not seeing much past the next twenty-four hours."

"Well, I hope at some point your next twenty-four hours include counseling and making things right with your wife."

"Renee..." Quinn began.

"Okay, I'm not going to push it. But it's clear I'm not going to be able to move any other request to the top of my prayer list. You're going to be staying right where you've been for the past six years." Renee looked sad for a moment. "Look Quinn, kidding aside. Well, I wasn't really kidding, you will be at the top of my prayer list, but a poor attempt at humor aside, you need to really think about what you're doing.

"Cassie doesn't deserve this. She has been through hell for the past six years never knowing if you were dead or alive. I can't even being to count the number of phone calls she made on your behalf, to the Red Cross and any number of government officials. Anyone she thought could help bring you home.

"She wept her way through most holidays and special events. She put up a strong front for Jani but at the end of each day all she could talk about was how you might have spent your day. It hurt her deeply to think of how you must be suffering. All she ever wanted was to have you home and here you are. Home. And yet she's hurting more than ever. Think carefully what you're doing, Brother."

Renee didn't wait for his response before she got up and left the room.

Quinn stood and walked to the front window. He stared out at the street, his hands shoved into his pockets. Sometimes it was hard to remember that he wasn't the only one who had suffered during his ordeal. In his mind, Cassie had been safe and sound. He had known the mission would take care of her and get her out of the country to safety. Yes, he'd known it would be hard for her with them being separated but he just never really realized what she had gone through.

What Renee didn't understand was that he was doing this for Cassie's sake too. He wasn't the man she had married. They both needed time to adjust to that. And what happened after they adjusted only time could tell.

He knew Cassie's heart was mission-oriented, as his had once been. Their whole future had been focused on their plan to spend the rest of their lives on the mission field. How could their marriage possibly work when one of them no longer saw that as part of their future?

The connection they'd had in their marriage had been physical and emotional but it had also been spiritual, strongly spiritual. They'd shared devotions and prayed together daily. With that connection broken, the physical and emotional connection seemed impossible.

Quinn braced a hand on the wall beside the window. He had no idea how to make things right. His heart just wasn't in it. In more ways than one.

The biggest problem for Quinn was that he couldn't see much beyond the next twenty-four hours. After six years of living day-to-day, hour-to-hour, looking beyond tomorrow was almost impossible.

*****

Resolved that her breakdown in the bathroom would be her last, Cassie left Renee's room. She had been spending far too much time crying lately. Somehow she needed to get control of her emotions and focus on what lay ahead.

As she stepped into the hallway she spotted Renee climbing the stairs. Cassie paused, waiting for her sister-in-law to reach her.

"I'm so sorry, Cass," Renee said. She gathered Cassie in a tight hug. "I don't know what's going through his mind."

"It's okay, Renee." Their embrace ended and Cassie stepped back. "If this is what Quinn needs right now, I'm willing to go along with it."

"How can you be so accepting? After all you've been through? I know your dream was to be a family again. This is just awful."

"It's certainly not what I had hoped," Cassie agreed. "But the most important person in all of this is Quinn. None of us have gone through what he has. I can't even begin to comprehend what it must have been like. I don't like what he's decided but there's nothing I can do but pray."

Renee stared at her, worry evident in her eyes. "Are you sure you're okay?"

"I have to be okay, Renee. Not just for Quinn's sake but for Jani's as well. She seems to be accepting this better than I am."

"Kids are resilient. I guess Jani is just happy to have her daddy near her for a change. Perhaps the questions will come later."

"Perhaps." Cassie shrugged. "We'd better go down before they come looking for us."

Renee gripped Cassie's hand as she moved towards the stairs causing Cassie to pause. "I'm letting Quinn stay here, I hope that's okay with you. He asked and I figured it was better he stay here than somewhere else."

"That's fine. I was pretty sure this was where he'd want to be."

"I'll be praying for both of you. Especially that Quinn will come to his senses." Renee squeezed her hand before letting go.

Downstairs they found Quinn in the den with Jani watching the video Renee had started. As Renee and Cassie walked into the room they both turned, Quinn with a wary look, Jani with a grin.

"I need to go to the house," Cassie told them. "Jani, do you want to stay here with Daddy for a while? Maybe he can walk you home when it's time for bed, okay?"

"Okay. Is Aunt Renee going to cook supper for us?"

"I'll make sure you don't starve, kiddo," Renee told her. "I think we can find something to fill that tummy of yours."

"Pizza is good," Jani said coyly, oblivious to the tension in the room.

"I think I can probably arrange that."

Cassie hugged Jani. "I'll see you later, sweetheart."

"I need to get my bag out of the car," Quinn said as he stood.

Cassie nodded and left the room. She sensed Quinn following behind her even though he said nothing.

She grabbed her purse and keys from the table in the hallway and headed out to the car. She opened the hatch and stepped back so Quinn could get his bag.

"I'll bring Jani home in a little while," Quinn said.

Cassie slammed the hatch shut. "That will be fine. She usually starts to crash around eight."

"I won't keep her out too late."

Awkward silence where there never had been before struck Cassie like a hammer. Was this the way it was going to be between them from now on?

Cassie turned to go to the driver's side of the SUV but a touch on her arm stopped her. She glanced down at the tanned hand before looking up to meet Quinn's gaze. Briefly she saw a glimpse of something in his eyes, but it was gone so quickly she wondered if it had just been her imagination.

Quinn dropped his hand from her arm. "Listen, I know this isn't how you wanted things to be and I'm sorry for that. I just don't know what to do about it. It doesn't feel right to pick up our relationship where we left off when so much has changed. I've changed."

"So where does that leave us?" Cassie asked. "Are you saying there's no hope?" Cassie pressed in a way she hadn't dreamed she would but desperation led to desperate actions.

Quinn looked away.

Cassie stared at him, trying to see the man he'd once been. If only she could will him back. The outward changes in her husband were a true reflection of his inward changes. He was completely different.

Finally he turned back to her, his brown eyes showing no expression. "I don't know where it leaves us. For six years I've dared not imagine a future. Now that I can plan one, I don't know how. I knew the man I was in the jungles of Colombia, but I don't know who I am now that I'm back in familiar surroundings. I need time."

"For better or worse, Quinn, that's what I pledged on our wedding day. Till death do us part. God saw fit to return you from your captives alive. I can only trust Him that it was for a reason."

Quinn gave a harsh laugh. "Trust God? I trusted Him and it got me almost six years as a hostage."

Cassie winced at the bitterness lacing his words. She quietly reminded him, "Job trusted him and though he lost much, he gained more."

"I'm not going to debate with you," Quinn responded, his hand slashing through the air. "You don't know what I suffered in that jungle. God left me there to suffer. I desired to serve Him all my life and in return He allowed me to suffer in a way no human should ever have to."

The bitterness Cassie had heard in his words before had been replaced by anger. An anger so unfamiliar to her. She had never heard Quinn speak in such a tone before.

As she stood looking at the stranger she was married to, Cassie felt a helplessness fill her heart. There was nothing she could say to pierce the wall around Quinn's heart. God, and God alone, would be able to work in her husband.

Cassie wondered how long it would take. She had waited so long already.

Before Cassie could say anything Quinn looked towards the house. "I'll bring Jani home in a little while."

Accepting that their conversation was over, Cassie nodded. "I'll see you later."

She climbed into the SUV and backed out of Renee's driveway. As she drove away Cassie glanced in the rear view mirror and saw Quinn still standing where she'd left him. She turned the corner onto her street and he disappeared from sight. Cassie wondered what was going on in his mind. She didn't even have a clue.

The house was strangely quiet when Cassie let herself in. Her breath caught in her throat when she saw the sign Renee and Jani had made and hung on the wall of the dining room. "Welcome Home, Daddy" was spelled out in big pink letters, Jani's favorite color.

Quinn should have been walking through the door with her. The three of them should have been spending their first evening in their home as a family. Instead, she was alone.

Cassie stared at the sign for several minutes trying to decide if she should take it down or not. Finally she decided that for Jani's sake she would leave it up. Quinn needed reminding of the fact they were a family and that his decision was disrupting that.

Turning, Cassie left and went to Jani's room to put her bag there. Over the next hour she unpacked bags and watered plants. Some of the plants weren't too bad so Renee had at least made an attempt to take care of them while Cassie had been gone. Cassie tossed out the ones that were beyond redemption and talked softly to the ones that still showed some signs of life.

With uplifting Gospel music playing in the background, Cassie began to relax. Working with the plants was soothing, even comforting. She sang softly as she worked, finding solace in the words of encouragement the songs gave.

With her plants taken care of, Cassie turned to the blinking light on the answering machine. She really didn't want to hear the messages there but knew she had to deal with them sooner or later. She grabbed a pen and paper out of a drawer and sat down on one of the stools at the counter by answering machine.

With a sigh she pushed the button to rewind and play messages. As each message played she made a note of it. Some were expected. Her pastor, her neighbor, Cecily. Some unexpected. Cassie wondered how the reporters had gotten hold of her phone number. It had been unlisted for several years now. She wrote down the information for the reporters, and then drew a line through each of their names. Come Monday morning she was getting her number changed. Wouldn't some of those reporters just love to get their hands on the latest twist in her little saga?

Cassie slid off the stool and stood looking at the list in her hand. She knew she needed to return the calls, especially her pastor and Cecily's. They were the ones she had confided in the most over the past six years. They had been there through the ups and downs. On more than one occasion they had encouraged her to stay strong when the news from South America had been less than encouraging.

But Cassie couldn't deal with their questions about the situation when she herself didn't know where things were going. She needed a few days to see how the situation with Quinn unfolded, then she'd call them.

*****

Quinn arrived at seven-thirty on the dot with Jani.

"Hi, Mama!" Jani greeted her with a big smile. "We had pizza for supper."

"Again? Leftovers?" Cassie asked as she took the container Jani held out.

"For you. Auntie said you probably wouldn't have eaten," Jani explained. "Have you?"

"Nope, I've been busy unpacking and trying to revive my plants." Cassie laid a hand on Jani's head. "Time to get ready for bed, kiddo."

"Will Daddy still be here when I go to bed?"

Cassie looked at Quinn.

"Yep, I'll hang around until you're in bed."

"Okay," Jani said. "I'll go get ready."

"Don't forget to brush your teeth," Cassie reminded her as Jani disappeared up the stairs.

Quinn moved to stand in front of the sign Jani had made. "She did a good job."

"Yes, she's pretty good at drawing. Better than I've ever been. Must have gotten that from you."

"I haven't drawn anything in years. I've probably forgotten how."

"I doubt it," Cassie said. "There are some things you just don't forget how to do."

Quinn nodded slightly. "Maybe I'll give it a try again."

"You can have the sign if you want. Jani made it for you."

"I think I'll leave it up here for a little while." He turned to look at her. "If that's okay with you."

"It's fine. I'm used to having Jani's work all over the house." Cassie put the container of pizza into the fridge, and then went to lean against the counter. Her hands rested, fingers laced, on the smooth countertop. "How is Renee?"

"She's fine. Funny it seems she hasn't changed at all in the six years I've been gone."

Cassie laughed softly. "Don't tell Renee that. She thinks she's matured. And to be honest, she has. At least she's not dating every bad boy that comes along. It appears she's outgrown that tendency."

"That's good to know. I'd hate to have to beat off guys so soon after my arrival home."

"Well, you'll still have to practice because Jani is growing up so fast. The boys will be knocking on our door before you know it."

Quinn shook his head. "I don't want to think about that just yet. Give me a few years. I'm still getting used to the idea of actually having a daughter. Don't bring boys into the picture just yet."

"I'm done!" Jani's arrival in the kitchen interrupted their conversation.

"Let me smell your breath." Cassie motioned for Jani to come to her.

"Aw, Mama, I brushed. I promise."

"How about we let your dad do the breath check this time?"

"Okay!" Jani skipped over to Quinn and motioned him down. She blew into his face and then grinned. "See I told you I brushed my teeth."

"Smells like mint," Quinn agreed.

"Good enough for me," Cassie said. "Let's head upstairs."

Jani grabbed Quinn's hand. "Let's go, Daddy!"

Cassie followed the duo up the stairs and into Jani's room. Quinn looked out of place in the frilly pink room. Jani's favorite toy, Barbie, was evident in every corner of the room.

Cassie suppressed a laugh when she saw the expression on Quinn's face. It seemed the fact he had a daughter and not a son was just really sinking in. There were no toy trucks or footballs for this little girl. She was a girly girl right down to her ruffled socks.

Jani climbed up onto her bed and slid between the Barbie sheets. "I want two stories tonight, Mama."

Cassie nodded and pulled the Bible storybook as well as her favorite book from the shelf next to her bed. She knelt beside the bed and felt Quinn do the same. Jani was learning to read so she enjoyed helping out with the easy words.

When the stories were read, it was time for prayers. Jani very seriously clasped her hands and bowed her head. "Thank you God, for bringing Daddy home. Be with him as he stays at Aunt Renee's. And be with Aunt Renee too. Help me to have no bad dreams tonight. Help me to be a good girl. And please give me a baby sister or brother now that Daddy is home. In Jesus' name, amen."

Cassie didn't look at Quinn as she tucked Jani in. Her daughter's simple request seemed very out of reach right then. It may well be a prayer that would never be answered with a yes. She brushed Jani's bangs aside and pressed a kiss to her forehead. "Goodnight, sweetheart. See you in the morning."

"Love you, Mama."

"You too, sweetie." Cassie moved aside so Quinn could kiss his daughter good night as well.

Jani's eyelids were already drooping as they left the room. Cassie turned off the light and pulled the door almost shut, just leaving a few inches of space so light from the hall could shine in.

Downstairs the silence was strained. Cassie knew she had to address Jani's prayer and she hoped she could do it without crying.

It hadn't just been Jani's prayer all these years. Cassie had hoped as much as her daughter to add more children to their family.

"About Jani's prayer..." Cassie began, struggling for words. "She's been wanting a baby brother or sister for a long time. I told her we had to wait for you to get home. I guess that was a mistake." Cassie ignored the pain that shot through her. "I'll talk to her about it."

Quinn shoved his hands into the pockets of his jeans and stared at the carpet. "I'm sorry to disappoint her."

And what about me? Cassie longed to ask. Wasn't he sorry to disappoint her too? Because while Jani was the one to have voiced the request, it was one Cassie had harbored in her heart for a long time too.

"She probably won't understand, but she'll accept it. She doesn't have a choice." Cassie knew she was being blunt but it seemed better than beating around the bush.

Quinn didn't say anything but continued to stand, head bent. Cassie wished she could read his mind.

"Are you going to go for counseling?" Cassie asked even though she figured she knew the answer.

Quinn shrugged. "I'll see. Right now I want to focus on getting other aspects of my life back on track. I need to get my finances straightened out. Get my license. I need to spend time with Mom and with Jani."

Cassie wasn't oblivious to the fact that she was omitted from the list of people he wanted to be with. It hurt her right down to her very core. Suddenly she was filled with a desperate need for his love and attention. And an overwhelming fear that she would never have it again in her life, that she would go to her grave never knowing what it was like to be held and loved by the man she'd given her heart to.

"I'd better go. Can I come by in the morning to see Jani?"

"Of course. I'd never keep her from you, Quinn. You're welcome to see her whenever you want."

"Thanks. I appreciate that. We have so much to catch up on."

Cassie walked with him to the door. Pain clenched her heart as she watched him open the door to leave. He shouldn't be leaving. He should be staying there with her and Jani. They were a family.

"Does it have to be this way, Quinn? You can stay in the guest bedroom. You don't have to stay with Renee." Cassie couldn't seem to control the words that tumbled from her lips. Pain forced her to try once more to get him to change his mind.

Quinn stepped out onto the porch and turned to look at her. Darkness shadowed his face so Cassie couldn't see his expression but she knew he was going to leave.

He lifted his hand and gently touched her cheek with his fingertips. "Cassie, I don't want to hurt you but if I stayed here I would hurt you even more than I already am. It's better this way. I'm sorry."

Quinn's hand dropped to his side and after a brief pause he turned and walked off the porch. Cassie stood in the opening of the door watching him as he walked down the sidewalk towards Renee's house. He never looked back.

Cassie slowly closed the door, locked it and then leaned her forehead against it. How long would it take for the pain to not overwhelm her every time he walked out her front door? How long before the state of their marriage wasn't a part of every conversation? Would things ever be "normal"? If only she could figure out what normal was supposed to be in this situation.

*****

The light from the streetlights flickered through the leaves on the branches above the sidewalk as Quinn walked slowly away from Cassie's house. The pleasure of just being able to walk was overshadowed by his conversation with Cassie.

He realized tonight just how much his decision was affecting her and even Jani, though she wasn't as aware of it. Quinn wished he could make things the way Cassie wanted. But he knew he couldn't even stay in the same house with her because the expectations would be there. The expectations that they would once again be the couple they were before he was kidnapped. And Quinn knew that wasn't going to happen. Too much had changed.

He turned onto the sidewalk that led to Renee's front door. Not wanting to go in right away, Quinn took the path around the side of the house to the back yard. The old porch swing from years ago still hung there and he sank down onto it feeling as if centuries had passed since he'd last used it instead of just a few years. He and

Cassie had spent many evenings on the swing talking and planning their future. It had been a favorite spot of theirs.

With a shove of his foot Quinn set the swing in motion. He looked out at the sky, the black canopy sprinkled with stars. He'd stared at a lot of night skies over the past few years. Never had it looked so wonderful. He was finally home.

The back door squeaked and Quinn felt the swing give as Renee sat down next to him. As much as he loved his sister, he wasn't sure he was up for the conversation she was sure to want. She'd held her tongue earlier because Jani had been there but now there was no buffer.

They sat in silence for several minutes, the squeak of the swing as it moved back and forth the only sound in the dark night.

Not surprisingly, Renee was the first to break the silence. "I can't count the number of nights I sat out here and prayed for you. I knew that somewhere you were probably looking up at the same sky. I prayed that you would be safe and that God would bring you home to us. It took long enough but He finally answered that prayer." Quinn could hear the emotion in her words. "I'm so glad you're home."

"I'm glad to be home. To be perfectly honest I never figured it would happen. When they finally told me what was happening I was sure it was a joke. I was positive they'd shoot me in the back as I was walking away. I don't think I really believed I was free to go until I got on that plane heading out of Colombia." Quinn knew he'd never forget the feeling of looking out the window of the plane and seeing the thick jungle and knowing that it no longer held him captive. Freedom! Something most people took for granted was precious to him.

Silence settled around them again but Quinn could feel the tension radiating off Renee as she struggled to not blurt out her opinion.

"I don't want to talk about it tonight, okay, Renee?" Quinn said finally. "I know you want to tell me what you think about how I'm handling this and you probably want some questions answered but I just can't handle it tonight."

Renee didn't say anything. Quinn looked over and saw her head bent down. "Renee?"

She looked up at him and in the dim light coming from the kitchen window he saw the tears on her cheeks. "I'm just so sorry to see this all happening. My heart aches for Cassie. In one fell swoop she got her husband back and lost him again. I know you have your reasons for what you're doing but Cassie's like a sister to me. We've gotten so close over the past six years. Even closer than we were before you guys left for Colombia."

Renee looked out over the back yard, a distant look on her face. "We held each other when bad news came, when we would hear there had been a report that someone had seen you killed. I was there holding her hand when Jani was born, when all she'd do was call your name in the midst of her pain. She refused all pain medication because she felt if you could survive the jungle she could survive childbirth. And she was so sure you were surviving.

"I saw the joy and the pain in her eyes when she held your daughter for the first time. I wiped her tears as she wept knowing that you were missing it all. The morning the call came about your release she called me so happy, so ecstatic about you finally coming home. She wept with joy that finally the man she loved with all her heart was coming home. You know what she told me? She said it felt like her heart was going to be whole again. That ever since you'd been missing a part of her heart had been missing too.

"So now what does she have? You're home and instead of having a whole heart, her heart's being shattered by the very man who was supposed to love her forever." The tears streamed down Renee's face even faster. "I'm sorry. I know you didn't want to get into this tonight. I need to go before I say anything more." She stood up. "Your stuff is in your old bedroom and the bed is all made up. I'll see you in the morning."

Quinn watched her walk into the house without saying anything. What could he say? In the past he'd been blind to the suffering Cassie had been enduring. In his mind no one had suffered like he had.

Quinn stopped the swing and leaned forward, his arms resting on his thighs. Staring at the porch floor, he thought of Jani and her innocent prayer earlier that evening. She had expectations for their family even though she didn't really know how things were supposed to be. She'd accepted his decision to stay at Renee's easily probably because she didn't know any differently.

What was he going to do now? He couldn't stand to see Cassie in pain but he didn't know if they had a future. How could a marriage work between a woman of faith and a man who had none?

Chapter Eight

The knock on the back door startled Cassie as she mixed up a bowl of scrambled eggs. She looked out the kitchen window and saw Quinn standing on the back porch. The shock of seeing him there so early froze her momentarily.

Conscious of the fact that she'd done nothing but run a brush through her hair and was still wearing the large nightshirt she'd slept in, Cassie went to open the door. She hated for Quinn to see her at anything but her best but she could hardly ignore his knock.

"Morning," Quinn said when she opened the back door. "Hope it's okay that I've come by."

"It's no problem. We're just getting ready to have breakfast. Have you had any yet?"

Quinn shook his head. "But I don't want to be a bother."

"No bother. I'll just add a couple more eggs. Come on in." Cassie stepped back to let him in.

As she turned from shutting the door, Cassie saw Quinn's gaze slide over her appearance. She was glad she'd taken the time during her long shower the night before to shave her legs. It was nerve wracking to have him see her in something that while modest, was still intimate wear.

"Sorry, I haven't changed yet. I'm still on vacation so I didn't take the time to get dressed."

"No need to apologize. If anyone should, it's me. I don't mean to interrupt your morning."

Cassie picked up the bowl from the counter and began to pour the eggs into the hot pan. "Quinn, you're welcome here whenever you want to come. For Jani's sake I don't want you to feel that you need permission to come by. I'll even give you a key to the house so you can get in if I'm not here."

"That's not necessary." Quinn shifted his weight from one foot to the other. "But I do appreciate you being so understanding about a situation that is not what you would like it to be."

Cassie shrugged. "It's out of my control and I've basically accepted that." After another bout of crying in the shower the night before, even though she'd promised herself she wouldn't do it again. "For Jani's sake I'm going to make the best of it. And it only makes sense that you have a key so that once I'm back to work you can get in if Jani needs something. Although Renee has one so if you'd prefer to just use hers that's fine."

Jani's arrival in the kitchen prevented Quinn from responding.

"Daddy!" She shrieked with delight and ran to him. "Are you here for breakfast?"

"Yep. Your mom said she's making enough for me too."

Jani nodded. "Mama always makes lots of eggs cause I love them. Not as much as pancakes though."

"Why don't you two sit down," Cassie suggested. "The first round of eggs is almost done."

She got another plate from the counter and set it in front of Quinn. "Do you want a cup of coffee?"

"No thanks. I kind of quit drinking it. The stuff my...uh..." Quinn glanced at Jani. "The stuff the guys made was always so strong and when I had some stomach problems it made things worse so I stopped drinking it."

Just another change, Cassie thought as she got glasses out of the cupboard. Quinn used to drink several cups of coffee each morning.

"Would you prefer juice, milk or water?"

"Juice would be good."

Cassie put the jug of orange juice on the table and then got the eggs and put them on Quinn and Jani's plates. She poured more eggs into the pan before joining them at the table.

"Aren't you going to have some?" Quinn asked.

"I'll get some from the next batch. Right now coffee is good enough for me." Cassie looked at Jani. "Do you want to pray this morning?"

Jani nodded and quickly launched into a brief prayer.

"Breakfast always seems to bring out the shortest prayers in Jani," Cassie said with a grin.

As she sipped her coffee Cassie found it ironic that Quinn had given up a habit she'd found. She'd never drank coffee when they were together. After she'd weaned Jani she had started drinking it. At the time it had been, in her mind, a connection to Quinn. As she'd sat drinking her coffee each morning and having her devotions, she'd imagined Quinn doing the same thing though they were separated by distance.

It saddened Cassie to think that this was just one more indication of how her heart and mind had created scenarios that were nowhere near reality. She'd imagined Quinn coming home and that they would have devotions together, sharing those early morning hours with only themselves and the Lord, and sharing the habit of drinking coffee. She'd even taught herself to drink it the way Quinn had, black.

Now she'd not only be not drinking coffee with Quinn but the likelihood of having devotions together was slim to none. Just one more disappointment.

Trying to hide the emotions that thought provoked, Cassie got up to check on the eggs. She listened half-heartedly to Jani's conversation with Quinn. Apparently Jani was giving the "I want a dog" spiel one more try.

Even though her appetite had vanished, Cassie forced herself to sit down and eat at least some of the eggs. Jani managed to polish off her plateful, as had Quinn.

"What are your plans for today?" Quinn asked when breakfast was over. He set the plates he'd cleared off the table onto the counter.

"I don't really have any," Cassie said as she put the dishes into the hot water that filled the sink. "Did you have something in mind?"

"I was wondering if it would be okay if I took Jani with me when I went to visit Mom."

Cassie nodded. "Jani loves to visit her even though she doesn't usually remember who Jani is. I'm sure she'd love to go with you."

"We're going to see Grandma?" Jani asked as she came into the kitchen with her plate.

Cassie took it from her. "Yes, Daddy wants to take you to see her."

"You want to go see her, Jani?" Quinn asked.

Jani nodded. "I love to see Grandma." She turned to Cassie. "Can I take her that picture I drew? The one of our family?"

"Yes, sweetie, you can take that to her. I think she'd enjoy it." In fact, Jani's drawings covered the walls of her grandmother's small room. They seemed to bring her a lot of joy and Jani loved to draw them so it was a mutually agreeable situation.

"I'll go get dressed." Jani spun around and skipped from the kitchen.

"I'd better help her. At least make sure she picks an outfit that matches," Cassie explained. "We'll be down in a few minutes."

It was more like ten minutes by the time they got back downstairs. Between coming to a consensus on an outfit and braiding Jani's hair it had taken a little longer than expected.

Quinn was waiting in the living room when they finished. "I just realized I can't drive there. I'm going to need to get my license renewed. Would you be able to take us?"

Cassie nodded. "As long as you don't mind waiting. I'm afraid it will take me a little longer than ten minutes to get ready."

"There's no rush. From what I hear, Mom's not going anywhere."

Cassie dashed back upstairs. She stood in front of her closet trying to decide what to wear. It seemed ridiculous to worry about it after Quinn had seen her in her pajamas but it did. Finally she settled on a pair of black jeans and pink T-shirt. A light coat of makeup, a quick turn of the curling iron, and she was ready.

The house was quiet when Cassie came back downstairs. She looked out the front window but saw no one so went through to the kitchen. What she saw stopped her in her tracks. All the dishes had been done and were sitting in a pile on the counter. Tears sprang to her eyes. That was something the old Quinn would have done. He had never hesitated to jump in and do what needed doing whether it was mowing the grass or washing the dishes. His thoughtfulness almost overwhelmed her.

Cassie took a few moments to compose herself before grabbing her purse and heading out the back door. She spotted Quinn and Jani over by the swing set.

They didn't see her right away so Cassie stood watching them together, all the while trying to ignore the little voice in her head that kept telling her that this was just the way it should be. She had to remind herself that this was the way things were at that moment but it was no guarantee how things would be in the days to come. Cassie knew she needed to remember that in order to avoid disappointment. She had to accept each situation individually and not set up expectations for the future.

Jani spotted her just then and waved.

"Ready to go?" Quinn asked as he and Jani met her at the bottom of the porch steps.

Cassie nodded. "As ready as I'll ever be."

The drive to the nursing home was short. It was one of the reasons they had chosen that particular home. But it wasn't the main reason. She and Renee had both loved the huge windows that let in streams of sunlight. And then there was the large fenced garden that had flowers of every kind and wood benches under leafy trees. The fence enclosed it so there was never any fear of one of the residents of the home wandering away while they enjoyed it. It was perfect for Quinn's mom who had always enjoyed her garden and being out of doors.

Cassie hoped that Esther was having a lucid day, or at least some lucid moments. It would give her such peace to know that Quinn was home safely. And it would be good for Quinn too, to be able to see his mom as she once was.

At the home Jani jumped out of the SUV and danced excitedly while waiting for Quinn to climb out.

Quinn leaned against Cassie's door, sunglasses shading his eyes. "Will an hour be okay?"

Cassie nodded and glanced at the digital clock on the dash. "I'll be back around eleven or so."

Quinn stepped back and took Jani's hand. Together they walked towards the entrance to the home.

Before pulling away from the curb, Cassie leaned her head on the wheel and said a brief prayer. "Father, I pray you will free the Esther's mind from the bonds of her disease even for just a few minutes. Please let Quinn have this time with his mom. For both their sakes." Cassie looked up and stared at the door through which Quinn and Jani had disappeared. "Amen."

She really did want Quinn's visit to go well. It had been hard enough for her to watch a once vivacious woman turn into a confused, almost child-like person. It would be even more difficult for Quinn.

Not sure where to spend the hour, Cassie ended up in front of Renee's bookstore. She parked the vehicle and headed inside. Renee was behind the counter working on a stack of books but looked up when the bell over the door rang signaling someone's entrance into the store.

"Cassie!" Renee left the books and headed for Cassie. "What are you doing here?"

"I just dropped Quinn and Jani off at the nursing home and had an hour to kill until they need to be picked up. I thought I'd come by and see how you were doing."

"I'm fine." Renee looked intently at her. "The bigger question is how are you doing?"

Cassie thought about brushing Renee's question aside with a casual response but they'd been through too much together over the past six years. Plus, Renee was the one person who had always seen through her mask of courage to the vulnerable, hurting person beneath.

"I'm doing okay." Cassie picked up a book and studied the cover. "It's not at all what I expected but I'm trying to just be grateful that Quinn is home and that he's safe."

Renee took the book from her hands and set it back on the display. Cassie looked up and saw the compassion in sister-in-law's eyes.

"I know. I'm grateful he's come home too but I'm also struggling to understand the person he's become. I don't think all is lost, Cassie. Don't give up hope. Our prayers brought him back home, our prayers will bring him back to your heart."

Cassie nodded. "I'm trying to remain hopeful. Sometimes it's hard but then at times, like this morning..."

"What happened this morning?" Renee asked. "I was surprised when he said he was going over there first thing."

"I was surprised too but it was just like we were a family, a real family, as we sat there eating breakfast together. And then..." Cassie's throat tightened. "And then he did the dishes."

Renee smiled her understanding. "Just like the old Quinn."

Cassie nodded. "It's like there are bits of the old him still in there. Maybe, just maybe, there's a bit of him in there that remembers his love for me."

"There's our hope, Cassie. Things like this will be our encouragement. I can't believe that God would have brought you and Quinn this far only to have things fall apart. I believe His plan is for you to be together as a family and will continue to pray and thank God in faith that that will happen."

Cassie hugged Renee. "I don't know if I've ever told you how much I appreciate your support and encouragement. I don't think I would have kept my sanity over these past six years if it hadn't been for you. Thank you."

Renee's eyes filled with tears. "You've been there for me too. I know we were close before and used to joke about being sisters even before you married Quinn but that is nothing compared to how close we are now. You are a sister of my heart. I love you, Cassie, don't ever forget that."

Emotions were simmering just below the surface and threatened to overflow but the ding of the front door interrupted the moment.

"Morning, Renee!" an elderly man called out. Mr. Norman was one of Renee's regular customers and from what she'd told Cassie, one of her favorites. "Has the book I've been waiting for come in yet?"

"It came in yesterday afternoon's shipment." Renee went back to the desk. "I have it right here waiting for you."

Mr. Norman smiled at Cassie as he approached the desk. "And how are you doing, Cassie? Heard that husband of yours was finally back on home soil."

"Yes, he's back and doing well. He and Jani are visiting Mom right now."

Mr. Norman nodded. "You be sure and tell him he's had lots of people praying for his return."

"We will," Renee responded. "But don't stop praying yet. There are still lots of adjustments going on for Quinn."

"Yep, I'm sure there are. Know a bit about that myself."

"Really?" Cassie asked.

"I was in the camps in World War II. Coming back to real life took a lot of adjusting. No one can really understand what you'd gone through except someone who'd been there. Some men were so changed they never got their lives back. Others had changed but wanted to be with their families enough that they worked hard at it. I'll be praying for your Quinn, Cassie. Just have patience with him. Things will never be the same but that doesn't mean they can't be as good."

Cassie nodded, understanding the wisdom in his statement. She had been so caught up in things being the way they used to be that she didn't see that although that was no longer possible, things couldn't still be good. In her mind it had been an all or nothing sort of situation. It was time to change her mindset.

"Thanks so much, Mr. Norman. I needed to see it from a different perspective and you've given that to me. I really appreciate you sharing your experiences and thanks for your prayers as well."

"If your young man ever wants to talk he's welcome to come by for a visit."

"I'll tell him," Cassie assured the older man.

"Now, let's have a look at that book, Renee, my dear."

Cassie moved away from the counter, leaving Renee and Mr. Norman to finish their transaction. She moved around the store, not really looking at the book displays, her mind totally caught up in what Mr. Norman had said. Just because it couldn't be the way it was didn't mean it couldn't be as good.

Cassie bowed her head and silently prayed, "Forgive me, Lord, for being so focused on the past. Help me to look forward and to be thankful that Quinn is back home regardless of how things are right now."

A verse slipped into Cassie's mind and caught her unaware, reminding her that God would carry on the work He had started in her *and* Quinn. Cassie knew the verse by heart. Philippians chapter one verse six. It was a verse she and Quinn had learned together believing that their marriage was a good work that God had begun in their lives and that He would carry them through. How appropriate that this verse should come to mind then. It was as if God was reminding her that He was still in control. He had brought her and Quinn together and blessed their marriage and would continue the work in it.

"Thank you, Lord," Cassie whispered.

"Cassie?"

Renee's voice interrupted her thoughts. Cassie turned and smiled at her sister-in-law. "I'm continually amazed at how the Lord works. He knew I needed to hear what Mr. Norman had to say."

"I needed to hear that also. I too, have been focusing on how things used to be. On how different Quinn is without realizing that I need to get to know the person Quinn is now and to accept that person.

"Oh Renee, my heart feels a little lighter now. You're so right in saying we can't give up hope. I will follow Quinn's lead and pray that God will guide him along the path he needs to healing and hopefully restoring our family. Not to what it was, but to what God wants it to be."

The two women embraced. Both had tears in their eyes when the embrace ended and they stepped away from each other, then they burst out laughing.

"We've got to stop crying," Renee said, smiling through her tears. "Especially when there are no tissues nearby."

"I better go," Cassie glanced at her watch. "My hour's almost up. My guess is we'll be back by here in a bit. I think Quinn will probably want to see what you've been doing with yourself."

"Well, stop at Delia's to get me a sandwich if you're coming back. It's almost lunch."

Cassie shook her head and laughed. "It's only eleven, Renee. Are you hungry already?"

"I didn't get breakfast and besides, it'll be closer to twelve by the time you get back here especially if you're stopping at the deli."

Cassie left the bookstore feeling lighter and happier than she had in days. She knew things wouldn't be easy and just because she'd decided not to focus on the past didn't mean that it wouldn't pop up from time to time but she had found hope again. It was a hope she was going to cling to.

*****

Quinn touched the sleeping woman's hand gently. "We're going now, Mom. I'll be back to visit again tomorrow."

Jani stood at his side and leaned over to kiss her grandmother's cheek. Esther didn't stir at all before they left the room. Quinn was discouraged and encouraged at the same time. He had been anticipating the worst and when he'd first arrived he wasn't sure Esther had recognized him but just moments into their visit her gaze had cleared.

She'd looked right at him and tears had filled her eyes.

"You're home!" she'd said and had seemed to know without a doubt that her son had returned.

The lucid moment hadn't lasted long but that brief time had allowed Quinn to see peace in his mother's eyes and know she was relieved he had finally come home. Even after she'd slid back into her world of confusion they'd continued to talk to her. Jani seemed totally at ease with her grandmother and the fog she lived in.

Jani had chatted cheerfully about their time at the cabin. She'd touched on the subject of the dog she wanted once again. Quinn was so glad Jani was comfortable with her grandmother. Cassie must have devoted a lot of time and energy to his mom and for that Quinn was grateful. Not that he thought Cassie would have neglected his mom but it was easy to allow busy schedules to get in the way of visiting someone who wouldn't really know whether or not anyone stopped by.

As they walked down the hall to main entry Jani greeted several of the nurses by name, just another sign to Quinn that she'd spent a lot of time at the home. They were just passing the last set of rooms when Jani suddenly released his hand and darted through one of the open doors.

"Jani!" Quinn hesitated to go after her, not sure he should be barging into rooms. He stood in the doorway and saw her talking to an older man seated by a table near the window.

"Daddy, come see Mr. Bill." Jani waved him to come into the room.

When the older man looked up and smiled, Quinn ventured into the room. It was an identical setup to his mom's except more masculine in décor.

"Mr. Bill, this is my Daddy," Jani said with a flourish of her hand in Quinn's direction. "He came home just like you said he would."

The older man stretched out his hand and Quinn took it. "Hi, Quinn, my name is Bill Stevens. Your daughter has been regaling me with stories about you for months now. I'm glad to see that you made it home safe and sound."

"It's nice to meet you. We were just here visiting my mom."

Bill nodded. "How is she today?"

"This is my first time seeing her so I have nothing to compare it to but I think she knew who I was."

"That's wonderful! Cassie says she has lucid moments although she can never tell what prompts them or when they're going to happen. I'll bet your wife was praying hard today that Esther would have one of those moments during your visit."

"Yes, I'm glad that Mom knew who I was. Since her decline happened after I was taken she knew that something had happened to me. I'm glad I could put her mind at ease."

"We've all been praying for your safe return. It's wonderful to see the Lord answer prayer. Of course we had hoped it would happen sooner but better late than never."

"I see you have a little visitor today," a woman's voice said from behind Quinn.

He turned to see a middle-aged woman wearing a nurse's uniform standing there.

"Ah, Vera, come to torture me once again, I see." Bill sighed.

"You love it when I stop by, Bill Stevens. Don't bother pretending otherwise." Vera set the tray she was carrying down on the table. Quinn saw all the paraphernalia for giving an injection and realized it was time to leave.

"It was nice to meet you, Bill. I'm sure I'll see you again." Quinn took Jani's hand. "Say goodbye to Mr. Bill. Your mom is probably waiting for us."

"Bye, Mr. Bill. I'll bring a picture for you the next time I come."

"You do that, sweetheart. You know I love your drawings."

Quinn was in awe of the caring and loving nature his daughter had. It seemed as if she radiated warmth and it touched anyone within her radius. Cassie had done a good job raising her.

As soon as they stepped into the main area Quinn spotted Cassie. She was talking to one of the nurses and had her back to them. The nurse must have spotted them because she said something and immediately Cassie turned around.

She smiled a big smile and Quinn felt his heart skip a beat. It was the first genuine smile he'd seen from Cassie since his return. Jani skipped ahead and Cassie bent down to hug her as she approached. When Quinn drew near she straightened and once again smiled at him.

Quinn immediately sensed that something was different. For days there had been a shadow of sadness in her eyes, even when there was a smile on her lips. Now there seemed to be a peacefulness about her. Her eyes sparkled as she smiled at him and the warmth he'd been noticing in Jani also radiated from Cassie. It touched the edges of his heart and Quinn felt something give within him. This was his wife. This was his family.

He didn't know what had happened within the past hour to Cassie but suddenly it seemed that her whole world had changed. Whatever his return had unbalanced in her life had been set right in the past hour. Quinn hoped that he was able to resolve his problems as easily but somehow doubted that would be the case.

Chapter Nine

"I'm wondering if I picked the right color," Cassie mused aloud as she looked at the house. She lifted a hand to her forehead to shade her eyes as she looked up to where Quinn stood on a ladder painting the trim around the windows.

He glared down at her and Cassie felt her heart melt a little. Quinn didn't smile much but the fact that he was glaring at her was encouraging. At least he wasn't walking on eggshells around her anymore. This past week had been a thawing, so to speak. Gradually Quinn had relaxed around her once he realized she wasn't going to delve into a serious discussion about their relationship every time they were together.

And they'd been together a lot over the past week. He'd continued to come for breakfast each morning and pretty much stayed right through until Jani's bedtime. Sometime he'd take Jani out to the park or swimming at the nearby pool. He'd done the outside work for her. Mowed the grass, trimmed the bushes and even washed the SUV. Pretty much the only thing he wasn't doing at the house was sleeping. Each night he still returned to Renee's for that. Cassie had accepted that it was what he needed to do right now, but she prayed every night he would change his mind.

"What do you mean you don't know if it's the right color?" Quinn demanded, interrupting her thoughts.

"I don't know. It's just a lot lighter than it was in the can. There's not as much contrast between it and the white as I thought there'd be."

Quinn sighed and climbed down off the ladder and came to stand next to her. He also lifted a hand to shade his eyes as he looked at the work he'd done so far. "Well, I told you I didn't know what you were thinking picking a shade of rose for the trim. Rose is for bathrooms or girly rooms. Not for the outside trim on a house. A nice solid blue would have been just fine."

Cassie was trying hard to concentrate on what Quinn said. Sometime during the past week he'd begun to wear his old cologne once again and as it mingled with his sweat, memories poured into Cassie's mind. She'd always heard that smells could trigger memories but she hadn't experienced it as strongly as she did at that moment.

"Okay, tell me again why we're painting this room in a hundred percent humidity and mid-ninety degree temperatures," Cassie said as sweat dripped from her nose onto the drop-cloth.

"You said you didn't like the color of this room," Quinn reminded her. "Today is my only free day for the next couple of weeks to help you out. We're almost done."

"You've got paint on your nose," Cassie told him.

"Do I?" Quinn lifted his T-shirt and rubbed at his nose.

It was the opportunity Cassie had been waiting for. Reaching over she drew her paintbrush across his stomach.

Quinn jerked the shirt down from his nose but held it up high enough to see the damage she'd done. "What did you do that for?"

"Couldn't resist the temptation," Cassie replied with a grin. She carefully set the brush down and stood, poised to dart away from him if he chose to return the favor.

There was a glint in his eye that told her he was considering it. "You shouldn't have done that, darling. You may end up with a room half pea green and half eggshell."

"I could finish it myself," Cassie told him confidently.

Quinn looked around the room. "I don't think so. You'll have to pay a price for this, Wife."

"A price, Husband?" Cassie grinned. "What kind of price?"

"Why don't you go get a cloth for me to clean this off and I'll think of something," Quinn suggested. "But don't think of abandoning me or the price will go up."

Cassie left and quickly returned with the wet washcloth. She handed it to Quinn but instead of taking it from her he grabbed her wrist and pulled her close. The wet cloth began to soak through her shirt.

"I'm getting wet, Quinn. Not to mention that paint is getting on me now," Cassie complained half-heartedly, enjoying the gleam in Quinn's eyes and the familiar scent of his cologne, her very favorite scent of all male colognes.

"You can just clean up the mess you made."

Cassie began to rub the paint off and really tried to resist the temptation to tickle Quinn but finally gave in and let her nails rake across his stomach.

"You are just pushing all my buttons today, aren't you?" Quinn asked as he grabbed her hands. "I'm never going to get this room done if you keep distracting me."

"I love distracting you," Cassie told him coyly.

"And I love being distracted by you," Quinn admitted. His gaze softened as he looked down at her and drew her close. "For the rest of my life you'll always be my biggest distraction."

"I'll take that as a compliment," Cassie murmured as their lips met.

"Cassie?" Quinn's voice broke into her memories, so familiar and yet foreign at the same time.

Cassie closed her eyes for a moment before turning to look at him. "What?"

"Where were you? I was asking if you wanted to keep going with this color or if you really did want to change it."

"This color will be fine." Cassie moved a couple of steps away from him.

Memories were still tugging at her as she continued to inhale that old familiar scent. Why couldn't Quinn have picked another scent to wear? She was trying so hard not to let the memories of the old Quinn overshadow her hope for the future with this new Quinn. Moments like that last one didn't help any.

"Are you okay, Cass?" Quinn asked, looking at her closely.

"I'm fine." She gave him a smile that she hoped was convincing. "There's absolutely nothing wrong with this color."

"You'd better not change your mind because this paint is supposed to be long-lasting and I'm not going to be painting this house again until it's chipped and peeling."

Cassie felt her heart leap. It was her turn to look closely at Quinn. It was the first time he'd ever made reference to the future, and even more surprising was that the reference seemed to say that he was going to be around when the paint started chipping and peeling.

"What's wrong?" Quinn asked again, this time with a little less patience.

"Nothing!" Cassie quickly replied. "I promise I won't change my mind. The next time it needs painting you can pick the color."

"You bet I will. I should have been able to pick it this time around considering that I'm doing all the hard labor," Quinn grumbled as he climbed back up the ladder.

Cassie gazed up at him for a few seconds, a mixture of emotions swirling within her. That brief trip down memory lane had left her feeling depressed but then Quinn's comment had filled her with hope. Maybe, just maybe they were going to be a real family one of these days.

*****

Cassie returned to work the following week, taking only two of the four weeks she'd initially booked off. She felt it was important to get back on their schedule. Jani would be starting school in another two weeks so it was a good for Quinn to spend time with her, just the two of them. Most evenings they did things together and usually Renee joined them. It was as close to being a real family as they could get without actually living together and for the time being, Cassie was satisfied with that.

Sundays were the most difficult. Cassie and Jani would attend their church along with Renee but Quinn had yet to join them. It was hard to field the questions about his absence without lying. Of course, the pastor knew the details behind Quinn's refusal to attend church, but Cassie didn't feel like going into it with the other members of the church. Instead, she just passed it off as adjustments that Quinn was going through and asked for their continued prayers.

Quinn hadn't started looking for a job yet but finances weren't really an issue. His dad had left him well off and Cassie had touched none of his inheritance over the six years he'd been missing. He had gotten his driver's license so he could drive Jani around now. At first Cassie was disappointed because his needing her to drive pretty much guaranteed that she'd be included in their times together. Fortunately, he still seemed to want her to come along although Cassie always waited for his invitation, never assuming she was included. Things hadn't progressed that far yet.

Time was passing quickly and it was hard for Cassie to believe that Quinn had been home almost a month. She'd been crying the last few nights but not because of anything Quinn had done but because her baby was going to be going to school.

The night before school started Cassie and Jani argued over what the little girl would wear for her first day of school. Jani wanted to wear her prettiest, frilliest dress to mark the occasion. Cassie tried to convince her otherwise, all the while holding back tears at the thought of her baby going to school for the first time.

Would there be other first days with other children? That was part of the pain. Jani's first day of school may well be the first and last time Cassie experienced it.

Trying to contain her pain, Cassie held up yet another dress. "How about this one? You always say how much you like it."

Jani cocked her head to the side and looked at the dress intently. "I still like this one better." Jani ran her fingers over the lacy pink dress she held.

Cassie sighed. She really didn't want to get firm with her but this was getting ridiculous. "Okay, Jani, here's the deal. You are not wearing that dress to school. I'm going to pick three dresses from your closet and you can choose from those three which one you want to wear, all right?"

Cassie saw a flash of rebelliousness in Jani's eyes but apparently she saw the determination in her mother's eyes because the defiance faded and she nodded.

Finally the dress was chosen to both their satisfaction. Cassie sent Jani into the bathroom to get ready for bed.

"Having fun?" Quinn asked as he sauntered into the room.

"Not really," Cassie admitted as she hung up the dresses Jani had rejected. She went and sat on the bed, the jean jumper they'd agree on in her lap. "I didn't think it would be this hard to have her go to school. It's not like we have never been apart before. We've been apart during the day since I work and we were apart when I went to meet you but this is just...different. It's a milestone, I guess. A major one."

Cassie could feel the tears welling up but didn't want to cry in front of Quinn.

"It's my first major milestone with her," Quinn said quietly. "It's not easy for me either."

Cassie had forgotten that. In the midst of her emotional turmoil she'd forgotten that Quinn hadn't been through the other growing up milestones. He'd missed her first step, her first word, the first time she'd said Dada.

"Yes, our little girl is growing up." Cassie sighed. Part of the emotion in this whole situation was not knowing if there would be any more children. She was suffering a baby ache in the worst way. It seemed every friend was pregnant; every co-worker was having a baby. She wondered if the ache would ever go away.

"You've done a great job with her, Cassie." Quinn sat down next to her on the bed. "She's a wonderful kid."

"Well, I've had a lot of help. Renee's been a great aunt and she got a good set of genes from her dad." Cassie smiled at Quinn wishing with all her heart he would take her into his arms so she could have a good cry on his shoulder.

"I'm done, Mama," Jani announced as she exited the bathroom. "Hi Daddy!"

"Hi, sweetheart. Ready for bed?"

Jani nodded and climbed under the covers. She snuggled down into her pillow. "Are you going to be here tomorrow when I go to school?"

"Of course. I'm coming over for Mama's great pancakes and then we'll all go to your school together. Sound like a good plan?"

"Yep!" Jani held out her hands and Cassie and Quinn each took one.

She prayed her normal prayer asking for the dog, the baby brother or sister but ended if off praying for her teacher and her new friends at school the next day.

"Sleep well, honey," Cassie said and pressed a kiss on her forehead.

"I will, Mama. You too." Jani gave Quinn a kiss and settled down to sleep.

When she'd been upset or worried about things when they were first married, nighttime was when Quinn would hold her and listen to her worries and then pray for her. How she longed for that. She didn't think she'd be able to fall asleep as quickly as Jani had.

"Do you need me to do anything before I go?" Quinn asked once they were back downstairs.

Cassie shook her head. "You're planning to fix the door tomorrow?"

"Yep. I'll have to stop by the hardware store after we drop Jani off. Can I drop you off too so I can keep the car and do a few errands?"

"I'm not going to work tomorrow. I figured I'd be too emotional and I want to pick her up from school."

"She's going to do fine, Cassie. For the past week it's all she's talked about."

"I know. I'm not half as worried about her as I am about myself. That's my baby going off to school!"

"You'll do fine too. Our moms survived sending us off, you'll survive sending Jani off."

Cassie hoped so. Quinn didn't see the bigger picture, the reasons why she was so emotional about sending Jani off. But in order to tell him about it, they'd have to have another relationship discussion and Cassie just wasn't up to it.

"I'll be by in the morning," Quinn said as he headed out the back door. "Try and get some sleep."

Cassie locked the door after him and then went to sit in the quiet of the living room. This was the hardest time of each day. It just felt so wrong for Quinn to leave each night.

For a few moments Cassie thought about letting herself indulge in a little emotional outburst but decided against it. Crying only left her with a sore head, swollen eyes and an aching heart. And most likely she'd be shedding a few tears the next day.

*****

Morning came too soon as far as Cassie was concerned. She hadn't slept well at all and needed more makeup than usual to cover the dark circles under her eyes. Quinn arrived in time for breakfast that once again consisted of pancakes. Jani had chosen the meal since it was her special day.

"Excited, kiddo?" Quinn asked Jani as they ate.

Jani nodded causing her braids to dance on her back. "I can't wait to see my room. Mrs. Theissen was really nice when I saw her before."

Cassie couldn't eat any of the breakfast since her stomach was in knots so she busied herself getting Jani's lunch ready. The brand new pink Barbie lunchbox had been Jani's first choice and it matched the pink Barbie backpack she'd also picked out.

"Guess we'd better go," Cassie said a while later. "Don't want you to be late on your first day."

Quinn carried Jani's backpack out to the SUV. Cassie locked up the house and followed Jani as she skipped down the sidewalk. Cassie was actually glad that Jani was so excited about school. It would have been harder if she'd been sending a kid to school who really hadn't wanted to go. At least it was only going to be hard on one of them.

There were lots of cars parked on the streets around the school when they arrived. Quinn, who'd driven the SUV, found a parking spot and the three of them headed inside.

Cassie spotted several familiar faces from church. Although the private school wasn't associated with her church it was a well-respected school and many from there sent their children to it.

Having come for an open house for kindergarteners earlier in the year, Jani knew just where to go and danced ahead of them into the classroom. Cassie smiled and said hi to a few of the people she knew and followed Jani into the brightly lit room.

"Hi, Mrs. MacIntyre, it's good to see Jani again," Mrs. Theissen said as she approached them, her hand extended.

"She's excited to be here." Cassie shook her hand then turned to Quinn. "Mrs. Theissen, this is my...uh Jani's father, Quinn." Cassie hesitated to introduce Quinn as her husband since she still didn't know where their marriage stood. She didn't want people to get the wrong idea. "Quinn, this is Jani's teacher."

The two shook hands while Cassie glanced around the room. Jani was circling the tables looking at the names that were taped to each table obviously looking for her own.

"I found my name, Mama!" Jani exclaimed, motioning for Cassie and Quinn to join her.

"I'll leave you to get her settled," Mrs. Theissen said with an understanding smile. She'd obviously been through more than one first day of school with kindergarteners. "You can hang her backpack over on the hook under her name. She can have her pencil box at the table with her."

Cassie thanked her and took the pencil box out of the backpack and headed for Jani's table while Quinn hung up her backpack.

Jani was sitting in her chair but didn't look at Cassie right away when she approached. Instead her gaze was on a little girl at the next table. She was a pretty little thing with blond curls and big blue eyes that were streaming tears. Her mother was trying to comfort her.

"Why's she crying, Mama?" Jani asked, looking up at Cassie with concern in her eyes.

Cassie knelt down beside Jani. "Some of the kids here today are a little scared. Maybe they haven't been away from their parents very much or maybe they're just scared because they don't know anyone."

"I don't know anyone," Jani pointed out. "But I'm not crying."

"Yes, you're being a very brave little girl. Maybe you can be friends with the kids who are scared."

Before Cassie could say anything more Jani stood up and marched over to the little girl and her mother. Quinn came to stand next to her and together they watched their daughter offer her hand in friendship.

"Hi. My name is Jani. What's yours?"

The other little girl looked at Jani, her tears momentarily stopped. "Amy."

"You don't have to be scared. I'll be your friend."

Amy looked at her mother who smiled encouragingly at her. "See, sweetie, there are kids here who want to be your friend."

"Let's go look at the books." Jani held out her hand and after a moment's hesitation, Amy took it. They walked off together, Amy looking over her shoulder at her mom only once.

"I'm Gladys Silver." Amy's mom came to where they stood and held out her hand.

"I'm Cassie MacIntyre and this is Jani's dad, Quinn."

"It's nice to meet you." Gladys turned to look at the girls. "I'm very grateful for Jani's offer of friendship towards Amy. I have to say we've been dreading this day. We've both shed a lot of tears."

Cassie gave her an understanding smile. "I've shed a few myself but it doesn't seem to be fazing Jani at all."

"I stay home with Amy so she's never really been away from me for any length of time. This separation is going to be good, yet difficult, for both of us."

"Do you have any other children?" Cassie asked.

Gladys shook her head. "Nope, I was lucky to have Amy." She looked from Cassie to Quinn and back again. "Is Jani your only child as well?"

"Yep. But I work so she's had lots of mommy-free time. You'd think I'd be used to it by now too but I guess not."

Just then a bell rang and Mrs. Theissen went to the front of the room. "I'd like to welcome you all to kindergarten. I understand that this can be a difficult time for parents and children alike so today you're welcome to stay until you feel comfortable leaving your child. It will get easier, I promise."

Jani had come back to her seat and was sitting primly with her hands clasped on the table in front of her. Amy was back in her seat as well and the tears were beginning to flow again. Cassie wondered if they could ask to have the girls at the same table but decided not to make waves on the first day.

There were two other girls and two boys at Jani's table. A couple looked teary eyed but none were openly sobbing.

"Mama, you don't have to stay. I'm gonna be fine."

Cassie wanted to weep at Jani's words of assurance. She glanced at Quinn. "Do you want to go?"

He shrugged. "It's up to you. Whenever you want."

As much as Cassie wanted to stay she decided to let Jani take this step of independence. "Okay, sweetie, Mama and Daddy are going to go." Cassie bent and kissed Jani. "We'll be here when school is out to pick you up, okay?"

"Okay."

A couple other parents were also making their way out of the classroom so Cassie didn't feel like she was the only one leaving her child right away. There were still plenty of people in the hallway as she and Quinn walked towards the main doors. Neither of them said anything as they got into the car.

"I'll drop you off and then head for the hardware store, okay?" Quinn suggested as he pulled away from the school.

"That's fine." Cassie was eager to be alone so she could shed the tears she was struggling to hold back.

After Quinn left her at the house Cassie went right up to her bedroom and threw herself down on the bed and let the tears come. It was so much more than it being Jani's first day and once the tears started, they didn't seem to want to stop. It seemed that her emotions regarding everything that was happening with Quinn were more than happy to lend themselves to the occasion and suddenly she was crying about it all.

When the emotions finally passed Cassie lay on the bed spent. She didn't know how long she'd been lying there when there was a knock on her door. *Quinn.* She really didn't want to face him right then. For some reason she was reluctant to let him see any weakness on her part, but she couldn't just ignore him.

Slowly she got up from the bed. Cassie rubbed a hand over her eyes knowing there was no way to hide the fact that she'd been crying. It would take some cold cloths and makeup in order to do that and there was no time with Quinn standing on the other side of the door.

Reluctantly she opened the door.

"Are you okay?" Quinn asked, concern evident in his eyes.

"I'm fine. Just needed to have a cry."

"The door was locked."

Cassie turned and walked back into the room. Quinn followed her and Cassie realized this was the first time he'd been in their room. Or rather, the room that was supposed to have been theirs.

"You don't have to lock the door to keep me out, Cassie. I would never barge in on you, disrupt your privacy."

Tears once again hovered near the surface. She wondered what he'd think if she told him that she wanted him to disrupt her privacy. She wanted him to feel comfortable walking into their room but right then it seemed that would never happen. Any optimism she'd held over the past couple of weeks was vanishing under the weight of the emotion of the day.

"I know. I just didn't want you to find me bawling my eyes out. Embarrassed, I guess." Cassie turned and saw Quinn looking around the room, taking it all in. She wondered what he thought of what he saw. She'd decorated it with him in mind but he'd never know that. The wall she was building around her heart to protect her vulnerabilities was getting thicker and thicker. If only she could read his mind. If only she had a clue of what he was thinking about their future.

Chapter Ten

Quinn looked around the room he'd never seen before. He'd been in every other room in the house but never Cassie's bedroom. Now that he was there, curiosity got the better of him. It was decorated in dark colors, burgundy and navy blue, not at all the feminine room he'd been expecting. It wasn't overtly masculine either but was a nice balance between the two.

He spotted their wedding picture on Cassie's nightstand. It was amazing that it automatically came to him which side of the bed was Cassie's. They'd been apart longer than they'd been married but he remembered that. He looked at the nightstand on the other side of the bed and saw a book there, open and face down. He couldn't read the title but wondered why it was on the other side of the bed if it was Cassie's.

Quinn glanced at Cassie and found her watching him. She looked at the nightstand and then back to him briefly before looking away, her cheeks flushed.

"The book is yours. It's the one you were reading the night before you were taken." Cassie walked around to the stand and picked it up. She stood looking at it for a few seconds before closing it. Without meeting his gaze she handed it to him. "You can have it if you want. Maybe you've been wondering about the ending all these years."

Quinn took the book and looked at the cover. It was written by an author he had once enjoyed but hadn't thought about in years. He ran a finger over the cover suddenly flooded with memories.

"Cassie?" Quinn leaned over to look at her.

Last time he'd checked she'd been reading a book too but now lay sound asleep curled up on her side. It was so unusual for her to fall asleep like that; she must have been really tired. Since he had an early flight the next morning Quinn decided to go ahead and sleep as well.

He put the book face down on the table next to the bed and switched off the lamp. Not wanting to wake Cassie but needing her close, Quinn moved over next to her and put his arm around her. Slowly he pulled her near, enjoying the subtle fruity scent of the shampoo she used. With her sleeping in his embrace, Quinn could finally relax and let himself drift off to sleep after saying a quick prayer for the activities of the next day.

But the next day had held terror. For the first time in a long time Quinn experienced again the deep heart-wrenching pain he'd felt at the thought of never seeing Cassie again, of never holding her close. The pain caught him off-guard. He'd buried it so deep after that first year he hadn't ever thought he'd feel it again and yet there it was, just waiting to remind him of how devastated he'd been. The pain had been so deep only because the love had been that deep as well.

"Um, I'd better get on with the door." Quinn handed the book back to Cassie. "You can keep this. I don't think I'll be finishing it any time soon."

He spun on his heel and left the room, and hopefully the memories he'd experienced there. It was all too confusing.

If Quinn had thought working on the door would distract him, he soon discovered he was wrong. Memories were flooding through the now open door in his mind.

Quinn wielded the hammer fiercely, trying to pound away the emotion. How was he supposed to deal with this twist? As long as he could keep the feeling buried, as long as he didn't feel the love, he could let Cassie go. It was the best thing for her. She deserved a man who stood by her side in all ways. He could stand beside her in all ways but one. Unfortunately, it was the most important one of all.

The hammer slipped and hit Quinn's thumb. Instead of getting upset, he welcomed the pain. It distracted him from the pain in his heart and the turmoil in his mind.

It didn't last long. Eventually the throbbing settled into a dull ache and again the pain in Quinn's heart came to the forefront.

How well he remembered the night they'd committed themselves to each other and to the ministry. He rested the hammer against his thigh and stared out at the street.

He'd picked Cassie up from the hospital where she'd just finished a twelve-hour shift as an OB nurse. Cassie hadn't been too tired so he'd taken her for a drive to the nearby park.

"I'm sorry I missed the meeting tonight," Cassie said, stretching from side to side before she sat down on the bench of a picnic table. "It was a long shift. I'd rather have been with you."

"The meeting tonight was great. It was a missionary from Africa that spoke. He was so powerful." Quinn moved to sit on the table behind her and began to massage her shoulders. "Last night's speaker was good but tonight, I don't know, this man just spoke with such emotion."

"That feels good." Cassie hung her head forward giving him access to the back of her neck. "Hopefully the speaker tomorrow night will be as good."

"I hope so too. Will you be able to get Saturday evening off so you can come to the closing banquet?"

"Yep. I switched shifts with another nurse today. I'll have to work Sunday in order to have the Saturday off."

Quinn continued to rub her shoulders and neck, wondering how to continue. He had something so important he needed to say to her. To ask her.

"Do you ever think you could be a missionary?" he finally asked.

Cassie nodded. "Ever since listening to the first speaker Monday night I've been thinking about it. I know they have a need for nurses in some countries. I've really been praying about it."

Quinn smiled. That was the answer he'd hoped for. He slid off the table and moved around to stand in front of Cassie. "I've been praying about it too. I really feel the Lord is leading me into full-time missions. There's a real desire in my heart to serve the Lord on the mission field for the rest of my life."

Cassie looked up at him and smiled. "That's wonderful, Quinn. I'm glad we're both feeling the same way."

"Me, too." Quinn dropped down onto one knee in front of Cassie and pulled the velvet pouch from his front pocket.

"Quinn?" Cassie's voice trembled.

He worked the simple ring from the pouch and held it up between his thumb and finger. "Cassie, would you do me the honor of standing by my side in service to the Lord?"

"Oh Quinn, yes." Cassie reached out and wrapped her arms around his neck. "I love you, Quinn. I want nothing more than to be your wife and to serve the Lord with you."

Quinn embraced her and then moved back and took her left hand in his. "I love you, Cassandra, and thank God for putting a desire parallel to mine in your heart." He slid the ring onto her finger and lifted it to his lips.

His heart rejoiced to know that he and the woman he loved would be serving the Lord together. Thank you, God.

Quinn lifted a hand and rubbed his chest. It had been an awfully long time since he'd felt such joy. A part of him really wanted to feel that joy again. The joy of the Lord. But it would require letting go of the anger he'd held onto for five long years. Anger at God. How could he ever forgive God for robbing him of six precious years with his family?

The anger began to build and overshadowed the pain. That was good, Quinn told himself. Focus on the anger, not the pain. The only thing that could ease the pain was to reunite with Cassie. And that wasn't going to happen because she needed a man of faith, and faith was something Quinn didn't have. And didn't want.

He lifted the hammer and pounded once again with more force than necessary. He couldn't have what he wanted. Cassie couldn't have what she wanted. It seemed they were destined to be unfulfilled.

Even though he was unwilling to let go of his anger, Quinn knew he did have to deal with the other trauma of the six years of being a hostage. For Jani's sake, he needed to get some help. He wanted to be able to put the past behind him and move forward with his daughter. He wanted the nightmares to go away.

They'd been coming with alarming regularity over the past couple of weeks. It was strange that after that first night in the hotel he'd had none but recently they'd begun to fill his nights.

He'd wake up in a sweat, heart pounding, sure he'd look around and find himself alone, behind the bars of his cage. Reality would soon reassure him that he was not in the cage. He had a comfortable bed beneath him. A thick blanket to ward off the cold. Four walls that protected him from the elements.

But he was still alone. He longed to feel Cassie's arms around him, her soft voice reassuring him that everything was going to be okay. But nothing was going to be okay. He was going to have to give up the woman he loved in order for her to live the life God had called her too.

"Do you want some lunch?" Cassie came out onto the porch where he was cleaning up the tools.

Quinn looked at her through newly opened eyes. He allowed himself to see the gentle, loving woman he'd fallen in love with and for a brief moment he was almost ready to tell her he wanted to move home. He didn't want to deal with the spiritual side of things. He didn't want to think about Cassie's calling to the mission field. He just wanted to be back with his family.

Needing to get away before he did something stupid, Quinn turned down lunch. "I need to do a few things at Renee's. I'll be back in time to pick Jani up from school."

"Okay." Cassie stood with her arms crossed, a confused look on her face.

Quinn wished he could tell her everything but he needed to do a few things by himself first. "I'll just leave the tools in the garage because there's still quite a few things I want to do around here."

"You don't have to do all this, Quinn."

"I'm enjoying it, to be honest. It's giving me something productive to do. Otherwise I'd just be sitting around on my duff getting bored." Quinn wiped his forehead with the sleeve of his shirt. "Renee has a few things she wants me to do too. A man's work is never done."

Quinn finished putting away the tools and then headed for Renee's. He wasn't sure where to start so he put in a call to the pastor of Cassie's church.

"Hello Reverend Stiles, this is Quinn MacIntyre, Cassie's… husband."

"Quinn, it's good to hear from you. We've been praying for you during this difficult time of adjustment. Is there something I can help you with?"

"Yes, actually. I need a recommendation for a good counselor."

"A counselor?"

"Yes. I'm sure Cassie has told you about what's been going on with me."

"She has come to me to share in confidence what was on her heart," Reverend Stiles confirmed.

"Well, I hope that you, in confidence, could recommend a counselor for me."

"There are a couple that I could recommend. I had given the names to Cassie before. Does she not have them anymore?"

Quinn cleared his throat. "Well, I'm kind of doing this on my own. Cassie doesn't know. I want to work through a few things myself."

"I suppose that's a good idea although I know she would be supportive of whatever you decided."

"I know. She's been nothing but understanding and supportive even when what I decided was not what she wanted. I want to do this now for our daughter. I know I need to deal with the past so I can move forward." Quinn hesitated, knowing the hardest part was coming. Maybe he shouldn't have phoned a pastor with this request. "I need a counselor that's willing to work on everything but the spiritual."

There was a long pause on the other end of the phone. "I see. Okay. Well, I'll still give you the names I would have given you before that qualification, simply because they are the best. You can make it clear to them what you do and don't want to discuss.

"I would really suggest Amanda and Steve Taylor as the best ones to contact. They've worked with several people trying to recover from traumatic experiences like yours. I think you'll find them helpful in your situation."

Quinn wrote down the names and numbers the reverend had. "Thanks, I'll give them a call and see if they have any openings. Are they the ones Cassie is using for her counseling?"

"No, I don't think she's ever met with Amanda and Steve. She had her own counselor, recommended by the mission, I believe." The pastor cleared his throat. "If you decide to go with Amanda and Steve, you can tell them I sent you."

"I will."

"Be sure and call me at any time, Quinn. I want to help in any way I can. Cassie has been an active member of the church and has helped many people. We want to see her, and you, happy."

After he hung up the phone Quinn sat and stared at the numbers, hoping he was making the right decision. He wondered if the counselors would be understanding of the limitations of what he wanted to work on.

The paper crumpled beneath his fingers. He closed his eyes and blew out a breath. It was just too much. *God, why did you allow this to happen? Why couldn't I have had these past few years with my family? Why did you take that away from me?*

Quinn opened his eyes and picked up the phone to dial the number for the Taylors. Fifteen minutes later he hung up the phone. He had his appointment but unfortunately, because he'd wanted to get in right away, he'd had to take an evening appointment since they'd just had a cancellation for that time spot. Otherwise they were full for the next week. Quinn had hoped he'd be able to do it during the day so he wouldn't lose any time with Jani but it looked like for this first appointment anyway, he'd have to take the evening appointment.

Cassie was subdued that afternoon when he picked her up. Jani, on the other hand, was bubbling over with excitement about her day. She rattled on and on about the friends she'd made, the things she had done and how excited she was for the next day.

Quinn was glad she'd done so well and hoped it didn't take Cassie as long to adjust to her daughter being in school. He also wanted to talk to her about the decisions he'd made and he didn't think he could do it when she was in such an emotional state over Jani going to school.

He hated that he was going to add to her distress but it couldn't be helped. In the long run it was going to be better for her.

*****

Cassie stared at Quinn. "You won't be here for supper?"

Quinn shook his head. "I'm sorry but I have to uh...do something."

Trying to ignore the sinking feeling in her stomach, Cassie nodded. She didn't want to think about why Quinn was missing dinner. He hadn't missed one yet since he'd been back. Every night he was faithfully at the table with her and Jani. And the fact that he wasn't telling her the exact reason for his absence just made her mind go a little nuts with speculation.

"I'd like to take Jani to McDonald's tomorrow for breakfast to celebrate her first week of school."

"I'm sure she'll love that."

"Great. I'll still pick Jani up from school and you up from work and take you both home. Can I borrow the SUV or do you need it tonight?"

"No, I don't need it."

"I'll just bring it back tomorrow morning."

"Okay." Cassie gathered her stuff and opened the door to get out of the car. "See you later."

That Friday was the longest day in history for Cassie. She was constantly thinking about why Quinn was missing dinner that night. She mentioned it in passing when she phoned Renee during her lunch break but Renee didn't have any information either.

Quinn seemed especially upbeat when he picked her up later that afternoon. Jani was disappointed when he told her he wouldn't be there for dinner that night but perked up at the mention of her favorite restaurant.

Cassie didn't sleep well that night and was dragging the next morning when she got up to get Jani ready to go with Quinn. She was toying with the idea of crawling back into bed when Jani and Quinn left.

"I have to wear pants, Mama, and socks so I can play there," Jani reminded her.

They finally settled on an outfit and then Cassie tried to braid her hair.

"I'm sorry, sweetheart but you're going to have to settle for a ponytail today. I just can't seem to braid very well."

"I wanted a braid, Mama."

"I know but if I braid your hair it's not going to look very nice because my hands just aren't working well this morning. You want to look nice, right?"

Jani nodded.

"Then I'll do the ponytail. You can pick a ribbon for me to tie around it."

That seemed to satisfy her and she sat still while Cassie worked the brush through her sleep-tangled hair.

"Morning ladies," Quinn greeted them as he came into Jani's room. "Not quite ready to go, I see."

"It'll just be a minute while I finish her hair," Cassie said. Jani handed her the ribbon she'd chosen and Cassie quickly tied it. "There you go. She's all ready for breakfast."

"Aren't you coming?" Quinn asked.

Cassie looked at him in surprise. "Me? I thought you said you were taking Jani for breakfast."

"I did but I just assumed you knew I meant you too." Quinn slipped an arm around Jani's shoulders. "Why don't you go get ready? We don't mind waiting, do we, sunshine?"

"Nope. You go get dressed, Mama. We'll wait for you."

Cassie was weary to her very soul and didn't know if she could handle spending a couple of hours in close company with Quinn. But there was that part of her heart that jumped at every opportunity to be with the man she loved, and it won.

"Give me a few minutes." Cassie hoped she could pull herself together in that short of time. Physically she was just not moving very well.

Ten minutes later she walked downstairs still not feeling very well put together but at least presentable.

Cassie was grateful for Jani's talkative nature. At least it meant she didn't have to try and search for things to say to Quinn. Instead she spent time watching him. He seemed different this morning but she couldn't quite put her finger on it. Happier, maybe. Relaxed, definitely. He just seemed more at peace with himself. Wherever he'd been the night before had worked wonders for him.

"So, Jani survived her first week but how are you doing?" Quinn asked as Jani ran off to play in the play structure.

"I'm fine. In a way it's not that much different than when she was with Renee during the day. It was just the thought of it all. My baby is going to school. Where did the past five years go?"

Quinn shrugged. "They seemed like an eternity to me."

Cassie nodded. "Yes, there were times it felt like time was dragging. But then when I have moments like this it seems as if they've just flashed by."

"Yeah, I know. I've missed five years of my daughter's life."

Not wanting the past to drag the morning down, Cassie didn't reply right away and then changed the subject. "What are your plans for the day?"

"I'm thinking of taking Jani to visit Mom, if you don't need the car, that is."

"No, I don't need it. Jani will be excited. She loves to visit Mom. How was she at your last visit?" Cassie asked knowing Quinn went to see her every other day or so.

"Same as ever. I don't think she's recognized me since my first visit there."

"It's hard to know when…if she'll have her lucid moments. Sometimes they happen when we're not there and sometimes we're lucky and get to see the woman she used to be."

"It's so hard seeing her this way. I'm glad she's not in any pain but I grieve for her." Quinn shredded the napkin on his tray. "I'm just glad that Dad isn't here to see her this way. I think it would have killed him. It must be hard to see the person you've loved change before your eyes. For them not to remember the love they shared."

Cassie could only stare at Quinn wondering if he heard the words he said. If only she could tell him that yes, it was hard to see the person you loved change, for them not to remember or acknowledge the love they once shared.

"Daddy, did you see me up in the tube?" Jani rejoined them at the table, breathless from her playing.

"Sorry, honey, I didn't see you. I'll watch for you if you want to go up in the tube again."

Jani danced off and was soon up in the tube waving at them through the plastic. Cassie sighed. "She makes me tired just watching her. I'd love some of her energy. It would be perfect if she had a little less and I had a little more."

"Are you not feeling well?" Quinn asked. "You look tired this morning."

"Didn't sleep well last night," Cassie told him, her eyes following Jani as she moved along the tube to the slide.

"Maybe we should have let you stay home and sleep," Quinn said. "But I'm glad you decided to come along."

Cassie was confused. Last night he'd had other plans, secretive plans, and then this morning he was saying he was glad she'd come with them. Her brain was too tired to figure out what it meant. "I'm glad I came along too. At least I didn't have to cook breakfast this morning."

They didn't stay too long at the restaurant, much to Jani's dismay. Once home Cassie started in on the chores for the day. She was tired and wanted to take a nap but needed to do the chores she'd let lapse during the week.

Lunch came and went with no sign of Jani and Quinn but Cassie wasn't worried. They had probably stopped to see Renee at the bookstore and she'd conned them into getting lunch for her.

A knock on the door interrupted her as she unloaded the dishwasher. She looked out the window and smiled when she saw who stood there.

Chapter Eleven

Quinn watched Jani polish off the large dill pickle she'd picked out at the deli. Renee leaned back in her chair and licked her fingers.

"Thanks for lunch, Quinn. I was starving."

Quinn shook his head in exasperation. "Why don't you pack a lunch?"

"I love deli sandwiches too much for that." Renee grinned. "I always seem to be able to con someone into picking one up for me."

"You have always been quite the con-woman. I'm glad to see that hasn't changed."

"Yeah. So much has changed and yet so much stays the same."

"We'd better go. Cassie's probably wondering where we are. I only told her we were going to visit Mom, not stopping to feed my con-sister."

"She'll understand," Renee told him with a grin. "She's brought me lunch often enough."

Still, Quinn didn't linger. He gathered up their stuff and soon he and Jani were headed for home. As they rounded the corner he spotted a truck in the driveway. His brow furrowed as he stared at it. He didn't recall Cassie saying she was expecting anyone.

"Hey! Uncle Blaine's here!" Jani shouted excitedly from her seat as they pulled up beside the shiny black truck.

Quinn barely had time to get out of the vehicle before Jani was opening the door and jumping onto the driveway. She took off at full speed for the back door. Quinn followed more slowly, a sinking feeling in his stomach as he wondered if this was the Blaine he thought it was.

He stepped through the back door to see Jani wrapped in the arms of a tall, lanky blond-haired man. Yep, it was the very same Blaine.

Blaine had been dating Cassie in the eleventh grade when Quinn had moved to town. It wasn't long before they were competing for most things in school, including Cassie's affections. Quinn had been the victor then, but suddenly he wasn't sure he'd win this go around.

"Quinn," Blaine said, reserve in his voice and expression. He moved Jani to one hip and held out his hand. "Glad to see you made it home."

Quinn wondered how sincere his statement was. A quick glance at the table revealed a nice cozy set-up with glasses of lemonade and a plate of cookies. It looked like he'd been there for a while already.

"I'm glad to be home." Quinn shook his hand, wondering how much Cassie had told him.

"Blaine is the assistant pastor at our church now," Cassie told him.

Quinn arched a brow. "Really?" Just perfect, he thought, a man in the ministry. It was what Cassie needed. What she deserved.

"Yes, I've been helping Reverend Stiles for the past seven years. I know it's a long ways from what I'd hoped to be back in high school but it's where the Lord has led me and I'm very happy."

"Married?" Quinn couldn't keep himself from asking.

Blaine shook his head. "Not yet. I keep praying but so far the Lord hasn't answered. There is one woman that has piqued my interest but alas, circumstances are keeping us apart."

Quinn felt like he'd been punched in the gut. Had Blaine been hoping he'd be declared dead so he could marry Cassie himself? Suddenly he didn't want to give up his wife. Even if it was the best thing for her, Quinn didn't want her to find another man.

"I guess that's the way it works sometimes," Quinn said vaguely.

Blaine bent and put Jani down. "I'd best be on my way. I have one more stop to make on my way home. I'm looking for a certain book."

He glanced at Cassie and Quinn felt anger flood him as he witnessed the wink Blaine gave her. Cassie grinned back at him, a mischievous look on her face.

"I'll see you tomorrow, Uncle Blaine," Jani said, tugging on his hand.

"That you will, kiddo." Blaine ruffled Jani's bangs before bending to give her a kiss. It was obvious they'd spent a lot of time together over the years. Would Jani like it if Uncle Blaine became Daddy Blaine?

Quinn pushed that thought from his mind. It wasn't going to happen, he resolved.

Together they walked outside. Quinn stood off to the side, arms crossed, watching as they said goodbye to Blaine and he pulled his truck out of the driveway. Once he was out of sight, Jani skipped off to the back yard to her swing set.

Cassie stood for a few moments before turning towards the house.

"I'll bet that's one man who wishes I'd perished in the jungle," Quinn said the words before he could stop himself.

Cassie froze, then turned to him, a shocked look on her face. "Why would you ever say that about Blaine? He prayed faithfully with the rest of us for your return."

Quinn shrugged; embarrassed that he was acting so juvenile. "Forget I said it. It was just a reaction to the years of competing with him."

"You have nothing to compete with Blaine over. He's a good friend, and I anticipate that continuing even though you're home. He'd be a good friend for you too."

Quinn doubted that but this time kept his mouth shut. "I'm going to mow the lawn. If there's anything else you want me to do, let me know and I'll try and get it done."

Cassie stared at him for a moment, then nodded. She disappeared into the house, tension in every line of her body. Quinn felt badly for letting his insecurities get the better of him.

What right did he have to lash out at Blaine? Quinn pulled the mower out of the shed and fired it up. The man had obviously been a great support to Cassie and was someone Jani enjoyed being around. Quinn knew he had no right to be jealous. Cassie had given him an open invitation to reunite their family and he was the one holding out. If he had anyone to blame, it was himself. He knew he couldn't have Cassie, and yet he didn't want anyone else to have her either.

Somehow, someway, he was going to have to work through things so he could have his family back. It hadn't been worth it until the moment he'd realized exactly how much he had to lose, and how desperate he was to hang onto it.

*****

The next afternoon Quinn was out in Renee's yard helping with her yard work waiting for Cassie and Jani to get back from lunch at the pastor's home. He was weeding the front flower garden when he heard a vehicle pull into the driveway.

He glanced over his shoulder, expecting to see the SUV but instead saw Blaine's truck. Scowling, Quinn got to his feet and turned to watch the man climb out of the vehicle.

"What do you want, Blaine?" Renee asked with a wariness in her voice that surprised Quinn.

Forgetting his own reaction to Blaine's arrival, Quinn turned to look at his sister. She stood stiffly, hose in hand, glaring at the blond man.

"Now is that any way to greet an old friend?" Blaine asked with an easy smile.

Renee didn't reply but moved her hand slightly causing the water from the hose to arc towards Blaine but not quite reach him. Quinn wondered about the animosity between the two and a grin tugged at the corner of his mouth. Part of him hoped that Renee did turn the hose on Blaine, but she seemed to be restraining herself.

"What do you want?" Renee asked again, still toying with the hose. Water arced in different lengths as she moved the hose up and down, never quite getting Blaine but coming close to his spraying his black runners.

"I know you love my company but I'm actually here to speak to Quinn." Blaine cast a look in his direction before looking back at Renee. "I wouldn't presume to hoist my unwanted company on you twice in as many days."

"Well, good then. I'll be inside." Renee moved the hose away from Blaine and stomped over to the faucet to turn it off.

It wasn't until Renee had disappeared that Blaine approached him. He shoved his hands into the back pockets of his faded jeans and stood looking at Quinn. "I'm here because I need to clarify something with you."

Quinn felt a tightening in his stomach. Was this where Blaine told him how he really felt about Cassie? He clenched the wooden handle of the small spade he'd been using to weed the garden. "Okay. What's up?"

"First of all, I want to let you know that Cassie never has, in the years you've been missing, and never will be, more than a friend. A good friend but that's it. I respect her and yes, I love her but only as a really good friend and sister in the Lord."

Surprise then relief flooded Quinn. But then another thought came to him. Blaine might feel this way but how did Cassie feel about Blaine?

"I appreciate you telling me this."

Blaine cocked his head. "I felt it was only fair to let you know. Even if I'd had any other ideas six years ago, which I didn't, Cassie set me straight right from the beginning. You were her husband and nothing and no one was going to change that. She's an amazingly strong woman."

Quinn nodded. "Even more now than before."

"I know you probably don't want a lecture from me so I'll make it short," Blaine said with a grin that quickly faded to seriousness. "Don't do anything foolish without first thinking it through. Your family has waited a long time for you to come home, don't throw that away without really trying to see if you can make it work."

Quinn felt a surge of anger. He wasn't sure who it was at. Blaine for interfering, or Cassie for sharing with Blaine.

He managed to hold his tongue on that subject but couldn't ignore the other one in his mind. "What is it with you and Renee? I've never seen her act like that before."

Blaine's mouth lifted in a lopsided grin. "Do you think I'm wearing her down?"

"Wearing her down?" Quinn asked, puzzled.

"I'm patient. One of these days she's going to come to her senses and realize what she's missing. Maybe then we'll be able to go out on our second date."

"Your second date?" Quinn felt like a fool repeating everything Blaine said but it was just such a surprise to him.

"Yeah, our first one didn't go so well. Renee's got some fool idea in her head that she's my second choice because Cassie married you." Blaine shook his head. "Cassie was my choice in tenth grade. I was a boy then. Renee's my choice as a man. What I feel for her is completely different from what I felt for Cassie fifteen years ago. One of these days she's going to realize that."

Quinn laughed then. He couldn't help himself. Blaine was suffering from unrequited love but it wasn't for Cassie as he'd thought, it was for his stubborn, hardheaded sister. It suddenly explained the joking exchange the day before when Blaine had mentioned going to the bookstore.

"Well, I'll see if I can help boost her opinion of you," Quinn offered.

"That would be great. We've wasted so many years already. We're not getting any younger, you know."

Quinn lifted an eyebrow. "How long ago was your first date?"

"It was just before you were kidnapped and Cassie came home."

"Ahhh. The timing wasn't so good, I suppose."

"Nope. Your getting taken hostage really put a crimp in my plans."

Quinn saw the grin on Blaine's face and knew he was just joking. "Sorry about that. If I had known I would have tried harder to talk my captors into letting me go sooner."

Both laughed and Quinn felt at ease with Blaine for the first time.

"Well, I'd better go. Renee's probably waiting inside to hear my truck leave. Don't want to disappoint her."

Quinn waved as Blaine pulled out of the driveway and drove off. Within seconds Renee reappeared.

"He's gone?" she asked, peering down the road.

Quinn wondered if there was just a twinge of disappointment in her tone. "Yep, he left. Nice guy, that Blaine."

"Humph," Renee said and swung around to pick up the hose and resume her watering.

Quinn dropped back down on his haunches and continued to pull the weeds, feeling better than he had in days.

*****

Things quickly fell back into their old pattern over the next couple of weeks. Quinn continued to come each morning to take Jani to school and Cassie to work and then he reversed it in the afternoon picking up Jani and then Cassie. He stayed for supper each evening so obviously whatever plans he'd had that one night had not been repeated. Of course he could be meeting whoever it was during the day when she and Jani were away.

Cassie knew she was driving herself a little crazy speculating but she couldn't seem to help it. Every day she waited for the other shoe to drop. Waited for Quinn to tell her that it was over. Each day it got harder and harder to think about that because Quinn was changing.

He no longer radiated tension whenever they were together and he joked a lot more with Jani and even with her at times. It was so hard to see the changes, the ones she'd wanted more than anything when he'd first arrived. It was hard to see him becoming closer to the man he'd been and yet still not have the marriage they'd once had.

"Are you going out for lunch, Cass?" Stef, another nurse in the doctor's office stuck her head around the corner, interrupting her thoughts.

"I'm going to pop down to the deli to grab something for takeout. What me to pick up something for you? I haven't phoned in the order yet."

"I'd love a really big dill pickle," Stef said giving her belly a pat. "It seems this guy likes the sour stuff."

Cassie smiled. "I craved the sour stuff with Jani, too. I'll add your pickle to the list."

After making the call to place the orders she'd collected, Cassie left the office. She made a quick stop at the bank before crossing the street to the deli. The small deli was an office favorite, but they tried not to indulge too often.

Familiar scents greeted Cassie as she opened the door and her stomach growled. Maybe she'd have to order a sandwich for herself too instead of just a salad.

"Hey, Cassie, your order's almost ready," Marie, the plump woman behind the counter, told her.

"Can you add a roast beef sandwich to it?" Cassie asked, leaning forward to look at the contents of the glass case. "I can't resist."

"No problem. Give me a couple of minutes to wrap it all up."

Cassie nodded and turned to see who else was in the deli. Sometimes Renee stopped by if the afternoon clerk arrived early enough. Her gaze skimmed the people sitting at the small tables. Not immediately seeing anyone she recognized, Cassie started to turn around but then something registered in her brain and she turned back.

There, sitting at a small table in the corner near the front window, was the last person she'd expected to see. Quinn. And seated across from him was a slender blonde wearing a business suit. She leaned close to say something to Quinn and they both laughed. Cassie felt as if a live wire had touched every nerve in her body. The pain was acute and intense. All her speculations crystallized into reality right before her eyes.

"Cassie? Here you go." Marie's voice broke through the haze of pain to reach Cassie.

Slowly Cassie turned. She tried to focus on Marie and block out everything else. She couldn't fall apart here. She needed to get out before Quinn spotted her.

"How much do I owe you?" Cassie asked Marie, surprised at how normal her voice sounded. She paid the amount Marie quoted and picked up the two large sacks and left the deli.

She didn't want to go back to the office now, but the others were waiting for her to return with the food so she had no choice. Could she possibly get through the afternoon as if nothing had happened? Could she possibly act normal when her whole world had fallen apart yet again? Actually, that moment in the deli had just finished what had started the day Quinn had arrived back.

"Cassie, are you okay?" Stef asked when she got back to the office. "You look beyond pale."

"I don't know. Suddenly my stomach feels kind of sick."

"Do you want to go home? I can handle things here."

Cassie shook her head. "I'm sure it will pass but now my roast beef sandwich is going to go to waste," she joked weakly.

"Nothing from that deli ever goes to waste. If you can't eat it I'll gladly take care of it for you." Stef peered into the bags and began to pull stuff out.

"Help yourself," Cassie told her.

"Let me know what I owe you!" Stef unwrapped the sandwich and inhaled with great relish.

"I'll go tell the others that the food's back here."

Somehow Cassie made it through the rest of the day. Quinn was all smiles when he picked her up making her heart ache even worse, if that was possible. How much pain could a person endure without dying? Cassie wondered.

"I'm going to cook supper tonight," Quinn announced as he drove them home.

"Really?" Jani asked. "You've never cooked before."

"Actually, I'm not really going to cook. I'm going to take you out. How's that sound? We'll even take Aunt Renee."

"Where are we going?" Jani wanted to know. "McDonalds?"

Quinn rolled his eyes. "I don't think so."

"Awww," Jani moaned. "I love McDonalds. I still need more of the toys. They have the small Barbie dolls right now."

"I doubt you really need any more toys, sweetheart. I was thinking more along the lines of a nice restaurant. I might consider pizza."

"Yeah, pizza!"

"Is that okay with you, Cassie?" Quinn glanced her way as they stopped at a red light.

"That's fine." Cassie had no appetite so it really didn't matter where they went.

"I told Renee we'd be by around five-thirty to pick her up."

Cassie wasn't so sure she wanted to spend the evening with Renee. If anyone could see that something was wrong with Cassie it would be Renee. They knew each other so well. Probably the best thing to do was head it off at the pass.

Once home Cassie went to her room and made a call. "Renee, it's Cassie."

"Hey, Cass. Where are we going for supper?"

"I think they settled on pizza."

"Sounds good to me." Pizza always sounded good to Renee.

"What's up? Change in the time or something?"

"No. I just need to talk to you for a minute before we picked you up." Cassie paused. "I've had a bit of a rough day and I'm not really feeling myself. I'd just as soon not discuss it later if possible. I wanted to give you a head's up so you don't ask about it at supper. I just want this to be a nice evening for us all."

"And discussing the fact that you're not feeling well would spoil that? What happened?"

"I'd rather not talk about it right now, Renee. I'm sorry but it's something I have to deal with on my own."

"We've been through everything together, Cassie. There's nothing you have to deal with on your own."

"This time I do. I'll talk to you about it later. After I'm not feeling quite so badly."

There was a brief silence on the other end of the line. "Okay, if you insist but just remember I'm here when you want to talk. Don't hold it in."

"Thanks, Renee. We'll see you in a bit."

A long prayer, two extra-strength painkillers and a quick shower helped Cassie to at least focus herself enough to hopefully get through the evening.

Renee gave her a curious look when they picked her up but thankfully said nothing. Quinn drove to a nearby pizza parlor and let them off at the door.

They had already been seated when Quinn joined them. He sat next to Cassie while Renee sat across from them with Jani. Cassie didn't know which was harder, having to sit next to him or having to look across the table at him.

They placed their order and then relaxed as they waited for it to arrive. Jani was busy coloring the kid's placemat they'd given her.

"I think I need to look into getting a job," Quinn announced.

"Really?" Renee looked up from helping Jani color. "What kind of job?"

"That's the hard part. I obviously can't just step back into flying and I don't really have any experience in anything else. I'm grateful for the inheritance Dad left because at least I didn't have to go right out and get a job when I got back. But I can't go on like this forever. I'd like to get back into flying but that won't happen right off the bat. I want to take some refresher courses. What do you think?"

Cassie really couldn't think of anything else that suited Quinn as well as flying had. He'd loved to fly and he had told her once that it had been his dream from when he'd been a child.

"Mandy..." Quinn stopped. "Um...a friend suggested that I write a book about my experiences."

Mandy. The woman in the deli now had a name. Cassie thought she was going to be sick. It was hard enough to have the woman's face in her mind but now she had a name to go with it.

"I think writing a book is a great idea. It would probably be a good catharsis for you," Renee said.

Cassie stared at Renee. She hadn't even seemed to pick up on the woman's name. Did that mean she hadn't heard Quinn's slip or that she already knew all about her?

The pizza arrived right then so the conversation ended. Cassie took a piece and tried to eat it but every bite sank like a stone to the bottom of her stomach. She sat and just picked at it hoping no one would notice she wasn't eating more.

Hope was not with her.

Quinn looked at her plate. "You're only having one piece? We ordered lots. Eat up!"

Cassie shook her head. "I'm not really hungry."

Quinn's gaze narrowed. "Are you on a diet or something?"

Suddenly the memory of that afternoon flashed in her mind and she saw Mandy sitting there, slender and beautiful in her suit. Maybe Quinn would have been more interested in her if she had lost those last ten pounds she'd gain with her pregnancy. Mandy had long blonde hair. Maybe if she hadn't cut those few inches from her hair.

"Are you?" Quinn asked again.

"Aren't women perpetually on a diet, Quinn?" Renee asked with a laugh. There was no humor in her eyes though as she looked at Cassie.

"Well maybe some women but Cassie never was and you certainly aren't," Quinn remarked as he eyed Renee's plate that had her third piece on it.

Cassie picked up the pizza and tried to take another bite and managed to get it down without gagging on it. She took a sip of her soda hoping it would wash it down.

"I'll eat more, Daddy," Jani said as she reached for another piece of the cheese pizza Quinn had ordered for her.

Cassie didn't know if she was going to make it through the rest of the dinner. Renee kept casting concerned looks at her. Quinn however, seemed oblivious to her discomfort.

It was with a sigh of relief Cassie shut the door behind Quinn a couple of hours later. She needed to be alone. She needed to figure out how she was going to get through this with her dignity intact. Without showing Quinn and the rest of the world that her heart had been completely shattered.

Chapter Twelve

Cassie changed out of her clothes into her most comfortable pajamas. Even though it was only nine o'clock she turned on the lamp beside her bed and crawled between the sheets. She didn't plan to fall asleep right away. There were some things she needed to think about and her bed was always the place she thought best.

Sitting with her back propped against the headboard, Cassie pulled her legs up and clasped her arms around her knees. She closed her eyes and prayed for the Lord to clear her mind. To help her view the whole situation with her mind and not her heart. Right now her thoughts were running rampant, making assumptions and her heart hurt more than Cassie had ever thought possible.

Cassie didn't open her eyes when her prayer was over. Instead, she focused on the Quinn she had known years ago, the one he seemed to be reverting to. That Quinn never would have gotten involved with another woman, even if their marriage had been on the rocks. Cassie was sure of that. She had to believe the Quinn she knew today wouldn't do that either. She believed that beneath all the changes there still existed his morals and values. Those morals would demand that he end their marriage before getting involved with someone else. Although she knew divorce was something neither of them ever thought would be an option for them.

Could she somehow bring herself to believe that what she'd seen in the deli had been a casual meeting between friends and nothing more? Cassie rubbed a hand over her forehead. Her heart couldn't seem to grasp that. Her emotions kept telling her it was something more.

But would he have chosen a restaurant so close to her work if he'd been meeting a girlfriend? He'd have to have known there was a possibility that she'd see them together. On the other hand, maybe he hoped that she would see them together and get the picture without him having to tell her. But that didn't seem like something Quinn would do. He'd promised to be honest with her and so far she thought he had.

Cassie knew that for her own sake she needed to give Quinn the benefit of the doubt. If Quinn did in fact have an interest in this other woman, he wasn't the man she wanted to have as husband anyway. Never had she thought divorce would be part of her life, and she herself would never pursue it, but there wouldn't be much she could do if Quinn decided it was what he wanted.

"Oh Lord, I know you're still in control of this situation even though it doesn't look really good right now. Help me to trust you instead of wondering about Quinn. I have to believe that it's Your will that our marriage be reconciled, that Quinn will renew his faith in you and have a powerful testimony to share. Give me the peace I need to see this through, whatever the outcome."

Cassie sat for a while longer, her head bent to her knees. She let the memories flood her. Over the past five years her memories had kept her going. Keeping Quinn alive in her and Jani's minds had sustained her. Now she called on them again in faith that the Lord would give her the opportunity to make more memories with the man she loved.

*****

Quinn showed up for breakfast the next morning. He gave her a curious look as he sat down at the table. "Are you feeling okay?"

Cassie glanced at him in surprise. She thought she looked better that morning than she had at supper the night before. "I'm fine."

"Renee mentioned something about you not feeling well last night. I'm sorry I didn't notice. I mean, I noticed you didn't each much pizza but I didn't realize it was because you weren't feeling well."

"I wasn't feeling great last night but I'm fine this morning."

"Glad to hear it."

Cassie set the French toast on the table in front of Jani and then sat down. "What is your plan for today?"

Quinn shrugged. "I don't have any great plans. Probably do a little work here and at Renee's. Did you need me to do something?"

"I don't think so. You've been working hard to keep stuff done up. I don't think our place has looked this good in years."

"Can we go see Grandma?" Jani asked.

"Sure," Quinn said. "I think that would be a good idea. Did you want to come, Cass?"

Cassie nodded. "It's been a while since I last saw her. I've gotten out of my schedule of visiting her. Maybe I'll make her some of those cookies she likes. Do I have time or do you want to go right away?"

"Go ahead and make the cookies. I'll do the mowing and once that's done we can go."

After breakfast Jani opted to stay and help Cassie make the cookies while Quinn mowed. It was right around lunchtime when they left. Quinn promised he'd treat for lunch after their visit.

Cassie could tell as soon as they walked into the room that Esther wasn't at her most lucid. There was the faintest glimmer of recognition when they walked in but then it faded.

"Hi Grandma." Jani greeted the older woman cheerfully. "We brought you cookies. They're your favorite kind." Jani put the container they'd brought on the small table and opened the lid. Using the napkins Cassie had also brought she lifted one out and offered it to Esther.

The elderly woman took the cookie and nibbled a small bite. "These are good."

Jani took a cookie for herself and climbed up on the bed next to Esther. "I helped to make them. They're your favorite." She leaned close to her grandmother and said in a loud whisper, "And mine too."

A nurse popped her head around the door. "Hi Cassie! I thought I heard voices."

"Hi, Sam. How's it going?" Cassie greeted the nurse. She was familiar with all the nurses in the home since she'd been making regular visits for almost three years. It was another one of the things she liked about the home. Low staff turnover.

"Do I smell cookies?" Sam asked Jani.

"Yep. We made them for Grandma. Do you want one? We brought lots."

"You know me, Jani, I can't resist those cookies." Sam helped herself to one. "I'd better eat it in here or you'll have a line-up outside the door."

"Hi Mom," Quinn spoke for the first time.

Cassie could see that it was still difficult for him to know how to act around Esther. She hoped he'd take his cue from Jani and just act naturally, talk to her about his day and what was going on. Cassie had held a lot of one-sided conversations with Esther over the years. And some that made no sense at all. But it made Esther happy to have someone there to talk to so Cassie just went with the flow. Jani had learned long ago that not everything her grandmother said made sense but that didn't matter to the little girl because she could always count on her grandmother to ooh and ah over her pictures.

Jani talked a bit more with Esther before sliding off the bed. "Can I go see Mr. Bill, Mama? And take him some cookies?"

"Sure. Why don't I go with you? Daddy can stay and talk with Grandma for a little bit."

It took them a while to get to Bill's room since some nurses and residents stopped them along the hallway to greet them. More cookies were dispersed but Jani made sure they kept some for Mr. Bill.

They were still there twenty minutes later when Quinn came looking for them.

"Sorry, we kind of got distracted," Cassie explained when she spotted him in the doorway of Bill's room. "Are you finished with your visit?"

Quinn nodded. "Did you want to talk with her before we leave?"

"I'd like to. Can you stay with Jani for a couple of minutes?"

"Sure."

Cassie headed back to Esther's room. The older woman was dozing in her chair and Cassie didn't want to disturb her. As was her habit she stood next to her mother-in-law and said a brief prayer that the Lord would continue to keep her healthy in spite of the Alzheimer's and that she would have peace even in the midst of her confusion.

They stopped by a restaurant near Renee's and got a bucket of takeout chicken. Renee's assistant was there working when they stopped to see her so they were able to convince Renee to come with them to the park for an early picnic supper.

It was a beautiful day. A light breeze stirred the branches of the large trees sheltering their picnic table. Jani played happily on the nearby swing set. Cassie leaned her arms on the picnic table letting the tensions of the week slide away. Whoever that woman was, Quinn was there with Cassie and Jani right then and not with her.

Cassie closed her eyes and laid her head on her arms. She could just drift off. Sleep actually began to tug at her but she was jarred out of her sleepy state by a beeping sound.

"What's that?" Quinn asked.

"My beeper," Cassie told him as she fished it out of her bag.

"You have a beeper? You never gave me the number."

Cassie gave him a smile as she checked the number. "This is my pager for Stephanie to get hold of me when she goes into labor. I told her I'd help her during her delivery."

"I thought you weren't doing deliveries anymore," Renee said.

Cassie looped her purse over her shoulder. "I'm not but Stephanie asked a special favor and since you and Quinn were both available to watch Jani I said I'd do it for her."

"Guess we'd better get you to the hospital," Quinn said as he stood.

They quickly cleared away the remnants of their picnic and loaded back into the SUV for the short trip to the hospital.

"Just call when you're ready to come home and I'll come get you," Quinn said. "We'll be at your place."

*****

Almost thirty hours later, Cassie finally left the hospital. Exhaustion pulled at her as she waited for the taxi she'd called. With it being so late she didn't want to disturb Quinn for a pickup. It had been a long and difficult labor and delivery. Stef had probably called her sooner than she'd needed to, but it was a first baby so her anxiety was understandable. In the end the baby had arrived safe and sound. At that point, she wanted nothing more than to climb into her bed and sleep for a week. Dr. Carlos had already told her to take the next day off and she planned to do just that.

Not only had the experience been physically draining but emotionally draining as well. As the beautiful little boy had slid into the world Cassie had cried. As she'd watched the parents huddle together over their new child, her heart had ached with loss. It looked like that special moment was one she'd never get to experience with Quinn.

She alone had cuddled their baby after she'd been born. She alone had counted fingers and toes. She alone had kissed the soft newborn cheek of her precious daughter and whispered words of love in her tiny ear.

The cab pulled up in front of her and wearily Cassie climbed in and gave the driver the address. She was tempted to lean her head back against the seat but figured she'd probably fall asleep.

Thanks to light late-night traffic they made it to the house in good time. She was surprised to see the car in the driveway. She'd figured that Quinn and Jani would spend the night at Renee's.

Quietly she let herself into the house and tried not to make any noise, unsure of where Quinn was sleeping. Was he asleep in her bed? Cassie hoped not because she wasn't in any condition to deal with that emotional discovery right then.

Moving slowly she climbed the stairs and was just going into her room when she heard a noise behind her. Thinking it was Jani she turned.

"How did it go?" Quinn asked, his voice rough from sleep.

"It went fine. They had a baby boy," Cassie told him, trying not to remember the many times she'd seen him looking rumpled from sleep. The T-shirt he wore stretched tightly across his chest and Cassie realized he was gaining back some of the weight he'd lost. He didn't look as gaunt as he had a few weeks ago. It looked good on him.

"Glad everything went okay. You must be tired."

Cassie rotated her head, stretching the muscles in her neck. "I am. It's been ages since I last pulled such a long stretch in the hospital."

"Want me to rub your neck?" Quinn offered.

Cassie's breath caught. No, she couldn't let that happen. Allowing him to touch her like that would take her memories down a path she'd been trying very hard to avoid. "Thanks but I think I'll just take a hot shower and crawl into bed."

"Don't worry about Jani in the morning. I'll take care of getting her ready for school. Do you have to work?"

Cassie shook her head. "Dr. Carlos gave me the day off since he knew I'd been with Stephanie the whole time."

"Good. You just take it easy tomorrow."

"I will. Good night." Cassie turned and went into her room and shut the door. She leaned her head back, her hands pressed flat against the hard wood. It was terribly hard to think of Quinn being in the same house and yet not sleeping together with her. Maybe it had been better for them both that he'd stayed at Renee's. Having him there that close, was more difficult than Cassie had imagined it would be.

She pushed herself away from the door and headed for her bathroom. That moment, being in such a highly emotional state, was hardly the time to think about their relationship and future. Only the worst would come to mind, and Cassie didn't think she could handle that.

Cassie peeled off her clothes and stepped beneath the hot spray of the shower. She knew she should make an appointment with her counselor. It had been far too long since she'd talked with her. She needed to talk to someone and for once Renee was not an option since this Mandy situation had raised its ugly head.

Water pelted her back, massaging away the tension of the past thirty-six hours. Cassie stood there until her skin burned with the heat. She turned it down a bit and quickly washed her hair and body before stepping out into the steamy bathroom.

Without clearing the mirror to look at herself, Cassie quickly towel-dried her hair then went into the bedroom to change into pajamas and climb into bed. She barely had time to say a prayer before exhaustion swamped her and all thought, pleasant or otherwise, left her blissfully alone.

*****

The house was quiet when Cassie woke the next morning. She stretched slowly, glad she didn't ache too much, and turned to look at the clock. Almost noon. It had been forever since she'd slept in so late.

Knowing there was no reason to rush, Cassie took her time getting dressed and doing her hair and makeup. Wearing a pair of leggings and a blue T-shirt, she headed downstairs to get a bite to eat. Her stomach growled, reminding her how long it had been since she'd last eaten.

She was surprised to see Quinn sitting at the kitchen table, a laptop in front of him.

"Morning," he said when he looked up and saw her.

"Almost afternoon, I think," Cassie said, suddenly nervous. It wasn't often it was just the two of them alone in the house.

"Did you sleep well?" Quinn hit a key on the laptop and it began to whir.

"Yes. I feel much better this morning." Cassie pulled a jug of orange juice from the fridge and popped a couple of slices of bread into the toaster.

"Hope you don't mind, but we peeked in on you this morning," Quinn said.

Cassie froze in the process of getting a plate out of the cupboard. "You peeked in on me? Why?"

"Jani wouldn't go to school without making sure you were really home and were okay."

"Oh. Well that's okay then." Cassie got her plate and waited for the toast to pop up. "What are you working on?"

Quinn leaned back in his chair. "I'm hoping it will eventually be a book, but right now it's just thoughts and memories of the past six years."

Mandy's suggestion, Cassie thought. She wondered if Quinn would let her read it before Mandy did. "David Warner wrote a book. I have a copy if you'd like to read it."

"I think I'd like to finish mine first before reading the experiences of someone else so I don't compare what I'm writing to what they did."

"That's probably a good idea. Just let me know when you want to read it. I have it upstairs."

The toast popped up and Cassie put it on her plate and began to butter it. The phone rang and she left the toast to answer it.

"Cassie?"

Cassie recognized the voice and smiled. "Hi Aaron! Long time no talk. How's it going?"

There was a bit of a pause. "I'm calling with some news."

"News? Has there been another release?"

"Yes. No one is a hostage anymore."

"No one? You mean both men have been freed?" Cassie felt Quinn come stand at her side.

"In a manner of speaking."

Dread began to form in Cassie's stomach. "Just tell me, Aaron. No more cryptic comments."

"Michael was freed this morning and is on his way home."

"And Kevin?" Cassie asked, her throat tight.

"His body was released with Michael last night."

"No. Oh no." Tears flowed. Cassie covered her eyes with a hand and tried to form words but all that came out were gasping sobs.

Quinn took the phone from her hand and spoke into it. "Aaron, it's Quinn. What's happened?"

Cassie made her way to the table and slumped down into a chair, her head buried in her arms. All she could think about was Kevin's wife, Mary Alice. How devastating it must be, to have waited all these years to have Kevin home again only to have him killed. It could have been her left to grieve Quinn's death. It could have been Quinn's body that had been left by the captors.

A hand touched her shoulder. Cassie knew she shouldn't turn to Quinn, but she needed his comfort, needed his strength.

Standing, she wrapped her arms around his chest and buried her face in his shoulder. His arms came around her without hesitation, and he bent his head to rest his cheek on her hair. They stood together for several minutes. Cassie could feel Quinn's heart pounding beneath her ear and the heaving of his chest that told her he was as upset as she.

Quinn's hand rubbed her back, offering comfort. Cassie didn't want to move from his embrace. For the first time since he'd come home they truly connected on an emotional level and were closer physically than they had been in six years.

Cassie lifted her head and looked at Quinn through liquid eyes. She was so glad, so very glad, that it wasn't Quinn who had died. Despite all their problems, despite the pain she was suffering, Cassie was glad she could embrace Quinn and hold him close. It must be so hard for Mary Alice.

Cassie knew she shouldn't, she knew it wasn't a good time, she knew it might lead to regret or even anger from Quinn, but it still didn't stop her from putting her hands behind Quinn's neck. She drew him down, rising up on her toes so their lips met.

Tears sprang afresh in Cassie's eyes as for the first time in six years she felt her husband's lips on hers. It was soft and gentle, a reacquainting kiss. Cassie wanted it to go on forever. She pressed herself closer to Quinn and tightened her grip around his neck.

When Quinn's hands grasped her wrists and pulled her hands from his neck, Cassie let out a soft moan.

"No, Cassie." Quinn stepped back from her. "This isn't right."

The air rushed from Cassie's lungs, and she felt as if she were going to throw up. Before she could respond, if she'd actually wanted to, Quinn strode to the back door and left.

Cassie stood alone in the kitchen, alone with her grief, alone with her longing to be with her husband.

This isn't right. The words echoed round and round in her mind. *Why wasn't it right?* she wanted to demand of him. He was her husband. She was his wife. It was natural. It *was* right.

Pain seemed to be coming from every direction. Grief and heartbreak flooded her. Cassie couldn't contain it any longer and fled to the sanctuary of her room. She crawled back into the bed she had vacated only an hour earlier and let the emotions overwhelm her. She cried for Mary Alice, for her kids and for Kevin's parents who should never have to hear such horrible news. She cried for herself and the heartache that just never seemed to go away. She grieved alone because there was no one there to hold her.

Chapter Thirteen

Quinn brought the SUV to an abrupt halt at a secluded part of the park. He got out and slammed the door with more force than necessary.

How could you do this, God? How could you let Mary Alice hold out hope for this long only to rip it from her at the very last minute?

Quinn tried to focus on the anger over Kevin's death because he didn't want to think about what had happened with Cassie. He didn't want to think about how right it had felt to hold her in his arms again and to kiss her. It had been like finally coming home. But he hadn't wanted it to come in the midst of such an emotional moment. There were too many things he needed to do before he had the right to kiss Cassie as her husband.

And right then, with his anger at God fueled anew by the news of Kevin's death, Quinn felt further away than ever from reuniting his family. His desire to find the faith he'd lost was squelched beneath the heat of his anger. How could God have allowed this to happen?

*****

Cassie watched out the living room window for Quinn and Jani. She was nervous about seeing Quinn after their encounter earlier but she needn't have been. Through the window she saw Quinn get out of the car but instead of coming with Jani, he stood beside the vehicle, watching her walk towards the back door. Cassie heard the door in the kitchen open and as soon as it closed again, Quinn turned and began to walk away.

"Mama?" Jani bounded into the living room.

Cassie grabbed her in a tight hug and didn't let go until Jani began to squirm. She let her go and smiled as best she could. "How was your day, honey?"

"Good." She dropped down on the floor next to her backpack and began to pull stuff out. "We have another verse to memorize this week." She held the paper out to Cassie.

Cassie took it and quickly skimmed the verse. When she realized what verse it was she went back and read it again more slowly.

Psalm 46:10.

It was the same verse God had brought to mind several weeks ago. Cassie read it again. It seemed God was reminding her that in the midst of this new turmoil, He was still God. He was still in charge. He was still there for them.

Cassie took a couple of deep breaths. She needed to keep her gaze fixed on Christ. It was so easy to allow the emotions swirling around her to take control and pull her under. He was God and there was no better person to trust.

"Where's your dad?" Cassie asked Jani finally.

"He said he had something to do tonight so he wasn't going to be here for supper." Jani didn't seem bothered at all by the fact that her dad was not going to eat with them like he usually did. "He said he'd see me in the morning."

And her too, Cassie thought. He had to take her to work so there would be no avoiding her the next morning. Maybe it was time to consider getting another car.

Cassie didn't feel much like eating the dinner she'd prepared, but for Jani's sake she tried to eat at least a little. After dinner while Jani was getting ready for bed, Cassie called Aaron to get some information on the funeral for Kevin.

"It's going to be on Thursday in Florida," Aaron told her. "Cecily and I will be going."

"I want to go too. I'm not sure about Quinn though. How is Michael doing? Is his adjustment going well?"

"He's been in counseling already with Susan and it seems he's doing as well as can be expected."

Cassie paused for a moment. "How is he spiritually, do you think?"

"Praising God for his freedom to anyone that will listen," Aaron said with a laugh.

Cassie felt a twinge of jealousy. Why had Michael managed to hold onto his faith? What had been the difference between their captivities to produce such different outcomes?

After getting the rest of the details for the funeral, Cassie phoned her boss to see if she could take some time off. He agreed so she phoned the airline to make reservations. She went ahead and booked two seats even though she didn't know what Quinn was going to do. She hoped he would come with her but knew it might not happen.

*****

The next morning Quinn arrived after they'd eaten already. Cassie hated that he was pulling away from them, all because she'd wanted to kiss him. It wasn't just hurting her, it was hurting Jani and that wasn't good.

After they dropped Jani off at school Cassie decided to broach the subject in hopes of getting things back to normal.

"I'm sorry about what happened yesterday, Quinn. It was just the emotion, the gratitude that it wasn't you who had been killed. It won't happen again."

Quinn pulled the car into a spot in front of the doctor's office. He crossed his hands over the wheel. "You don't need to apologize, Cassie. I think I need to apologize for leaving like I did. It's just...I don't want to jump right into...that when there's so many other things that are demanding our attention."

"I guess it's just best if we both just agree to forget about it." Even as she said it, Cassie knew she'd never forget it. Her first real physical contact with her husband after nearly six years and she was supposed to just forget about it? Cassie didn't think so, but for Quinn's sake she'd say she would.

"Yeah, it's probably best if we do," Quinn agreed.

"This Thursday is Kevin's funeral. I'm planning to go. Would you like to go with me?"

Quinn was quiet for a few moments. "Sure. It would be good to see the others."

Cassie was glad he'd agreed. Maybe meeting the others would give him a different perspective on his situation.

The day went better than she'd anticipated. Five o'clock rolled around before she knew it. As she got her things together she was surprised to see Quinn walk into the office. Usually he just waited for her in the SUV.

"Ready to go?"

"Am I that late?" Cassie asked as she turned off the computer and picked up her purse.

"No. I just thought I'd come in and see where you work."

"Well, this is it." Cassie waved her hand around the now empty room. It hadn't been so quiet a couple of hours earlier when several mothers had been there with their rambunctious children. "I really enjoy the work here, and Dr. Carlos is great to work for."

"I'm surprised you're not working in the hospital."

"I did think about it but the hours here were more stable and Dr. Carlos was very understanding of my role as single mom."

"I'm sorry you had to deal with that. I wish I could have been here for you and Jani."

Cassie smiled at him. "You're here now. Regrets won't do you a lot of good, particularly when they're for something you had no control over."

"You're right but every day I'm with Jani I realize just how much I've missed."

Cassie called good night to Dr. Carlos before leading Quinn out the front door. She turned her key in the lock. "Yes, you've missed the first five years of Jani's life but look at how much still lies ahead. And she doesn't remember most of the years you were away. If she were older she'd be more aware of the time you'd missed. And right now she's just glad to have you home."

Quinn opened the car door for her and waited for her to get in before shutting it. He rounded the front of the vehicle and climbed in the driver's side. "I know you're right, but it's still hard to think about what I've missed."

Cassie stared out the side window. Did he think about what he'd missed in their marriage too, or just what he'd missed with Jani?

Quinn swung the SUV into a spot in front of Renee's store. Cassie got out and followed him in. Jani was perched on a stool behind the counter talking to one of the customers.
Cassie almost ran into Quinn when he stopped abruptly.

"What's wrong?"

"Nothing. I'm just once again amazed by Jani."

Cassie stepped beside him and looked to where Jani sat. "She loves coming to the store."

"You've done such a great job with her. I know I've said that before but I really mean it." Quinn glanced down at her. "She is comfortable with young kids and with old people like Mom and Mr. Bill. She's outgoing and polite."

Cassie laughed. "Don't make her out to be too perfect. She has her faults although most of them usually manifest themselves at home. She can be downright stubborn at times, but she is rarely willfully disobedient for which I'm very thankful."

"You obviously didn't need me around to help raise her. You did such a great job on your own."

"I needed you. I still need you, as a father for her. Once of these days she's going to start spreading her wings and testing her boundaries and I think it will take both of us to keep things under control."

"Hey, guys!" Renee called from behind the counter and motioned them over.

"Hi, Mama," Jani said as she held out her arms for a hug without getting down from the stool.

"Helping Aunt Renee out?" Cassie asked.

"Yep. I get to put the books into the bag unless they're too heavy, then Auntie does it."

"Well, we'd better head for home so I can get supper on."

Jani protested but knew better than to push the issue and soon hopped off the stool. "See you tomorrow, Auntie."

"You bet, kiddo." Renee fished in her pockets and then held out a quarter. "Here's your pay for a job well done."

Jani grinned as she took the money. Cassie knew it would go right into her bank at home. Her dog-shaped bank was slowing filling with money that Jani hoped to buy a dog with some day.

"Did Quinn talk to you about watching Jani for a couple of days?" Cassie asked.

Renee nodded. "It will be fine. I just wish the news had been better about Kevin. How terrible."

"Yeah, it was hard to hear. It could have been Quinn. That's the thought that keeps playing in my mind."

Renee gave her a hug. "But it wasn't. He's home and healthy."

"Yes, and I'm very thankful for that. God was good to us." Cassie glanced out the window of the store and saw Quinn and Jani waiting in the van. "I'd better go. See you tomorrow."

Once home it didn't take Cassie long to get supper on the table since she'd started it in the slow cooker earlier in the day. The rest of the evening followed its predictable schedule but instead of leaving right away Quinn hung around.

"I wonder if Michael and Susan will be at the funeral," Quinn said as he sat down on one of the stools at the counter.

"I wouldn't be surprised. Aaron and Cecily are going to be there." Cassie put the last plate in the dishwasher. "I think there are going to be a lot of people at the funeral. This situation has gotten a lot of publicity over the years."

She wondered if she should tell Quinn that Michael had not lost his faith during his years of captivity. In fact, from what Aaron had said, his faith was as strong as ever.

Quinn stood. "I'd better go."

Cassie followed him to the front door to say good night. She realized she hadn't picked up the mail so pulled it out of the box. On the very top was a thick padded envelope addressed to Quinn.

"Quinn," Cassie called out to him since he hadn't gone too far down the sidewalk.

He turned back and Cassie ran down the steps toward him. "This is addressed to you."

Quinn took it and looked at the address. A frown furrowed his brow. "I wasn't expecting anything. Thanks."

Cassie wondered what was in it but didn't press. "See you in the morning."

Quinn walked slowly home, the package in his hand. It was from Ben Locke, the mission director. What could he be sending him?

At the house he found Renee in the dining room, papers spread all around her.

"Hi, Sis." Quinn sat down on a chair across from her.

Renee looked up and shoved her wire rim glasses onto the top of her head. "How're you doing?"

"I'm fine." Quinn fiddled with the package in his hands. "I'm not really looking forward to the funeral but then I guess funerals aren't something you're supposed to be excited about."

"Nope, not unless you hated the person."

"Which I didn't."

"I think it will be good for you and Cassie to spend some time alone together."

Quinn waited for the automatic denial to spring to his lips but it didn't. "Yeah, maybe it will be good."

Renee arched a brow. Obviously she'd been anticipating his denial as well. "Something you want to talk about?"

Quinn shook his head. "Not right now." He stood up. "I'm going to bed."

"See you in the morning." Renee pulled the glasses back down onto her nose and returned her attention to the papers spread before her.

Upstairs, Quinn tossed the package onto his bed as he walked past it to the bathroom. For some reason he was reluctant to open it.

There was so much on his mind. The news of Kevin's death, the funeral, the package, the kiss...especially the kiss. He didn't know what to do. Cassie said to forget it but it just wasn't going to happen. If he had been released the first year, that kiss would have been what their reunion would have been like. Instead it had been stiff and emotionless. Flat.

Quinn walked to the window and stared out at the black sky. "Okay God, I need help. I don't know what to do. I don't want to hurt Cassie but I need her in my life. I need a miracle here. For years I've felt You abandoned me in that jungle. But I did get out. Kevin didn't. Maybe that's my miracle. Just surviving to tell the story is my miracle.

"If I could just understand why; why You let me spend six years as a hostage. You had a reason for Joseph when he was abandoned by his family and ended up in jail. You gave back to Job more than you'd taken. What is it for me, Lord? Why did You let this happen to me?"

Quinn gave up waiting for an answer. He changed into a pair of shorts and a T-shirt and brushed his teeth. The bed sank a bit as he lay down and stretched out his legs. He reached over and dimmed the light but didn't turn it right off, and tried to fall asleep. The next day was going to be difficult and he wanted to be well rested.

Unfortunately, sleep wasn't coming. Quinn heard Renee come upstairs to get ready for bed. Soon the house was quiet but still sleep didn't come.

First his back, then his stomach. One side and then the other. Finally Quinn gave up and swung his legs over the side of the bed. He sat up and sighed. Not knowing what else to do, Quinn picked up the package and quickly tore one end open. He dumped the contents onto the bed. There was a piece of paper, a small white padded envelope and a DVD.

Quinn picked up the paper and opened it.

"Quinn, This DVD was given to me by a missionary with another mission who had an incredible meeting with someone who had some contact with you. I think you'll find the story on this videotape amazing. If you haven't already opened the other smaller envelope, please wait until after you watch the video. I think it will hold more meaning that way. You are continually in our thoughts and prayers."

Ben Locke had signed it. Quinn read it again, wondering what on earth it could mean. He picked up the DVD and the envelope. Since he couldn't sleep anyway, Quinn decided to watch the DVD. He got out of bed and went to the small desk where his laptop sat. In the dimly lit room, he put the disk in and sat back to watch it.

The first voice he heard caused his stomach to knot and perspiration to bead on his forehead. He reached for the touch pad to turn it off, but then began to listen to what the man was saying. It was in Spanish, but he could understand most of it having become quite fluent by the end of his captivity.

Suddenly another man appeared on the screen. The missionary.

"Hello, Quinn. My name is Andrew Hill and I have someone here who has a story to tell you. I'm not sure how much Spanish you know, so I'll be translating for him.

"To start back a bit, Lito came to me earlier this week wanting to know if I knew you. Of course we've never met, but I did know of you, had prayed for you, in fact. I agreed to help him get in contact with you because his story is absolutely amazing."

Quinn looked at the man sitting next to the missionary. He had been one of the men who'd kidnapped the four missionaries. When the group had separated, he'd been the leader of the men who'd taken Quinn. He couldn't imagine that this man had anything good to say. He hadn't been the worst of the captors, in fact, he'd probably been one of the better ones but still...he'd been a captor.

Curiosity kept Quinn from stopping the DVD. Over the next hour, Quinn had to admit the story he heard was as amazing as the missionary had said it would be. After that first year, Lito had been replaced as the leader of the group, and Quinn had never known what had happened to him. Because his faith had still been strong, Quinn had tried to witness to him in the time before he'd left. It had been hard because of the language barrier but he'd tried and obviously he'd gotten through.

Lito had returned to his home village, planning to take up the farming he'd left behind to join the rebels. But deep inside him was a longing to know more about what Quinn had shared. He had left his family again and gone to other villages searching for someone who could give him answers. He found a pastor in a larger village who shared the gospel with him again and led him the Lord.

Over the next few months, Lito moved his family to that village so he could learn from the pastor. Finally he had moved back to his own village and began to share the gospel there and had even started a small church.

Is this why, Lord? Quinn asked. He was glad Lito had known him at the beginning of his captivity and not at the end. Guilt speared him.

Perhaps God had placed him in the middle of those men to share the gospel so that as it got more dangerous for missionaries to remain in that area, there would still be seeds planted that would hopefully grow and flourish like they had in Lito's situation.

Tears filled Quinn's eyes and a sense of failure settled over him like a thick cape of darkness. The Lord had sent him into a hostile mission field and because it hadn't been where he'd thought the Lord had wanted him, doing what he'd trained to do, he'd rebelled. Instead of taking advantage of being with those men twenty-four hours a day and sharing the gospel with them regularly, he'd retreated into a rebellious silence.

Quinn focused on the screen, looking at the man who had taken a seed planted by him and had not only allowed it to flourish but had planted seeds of his own. How many more would have been saved if Quinn had only managed to remain true to his convictions instead of turning away from God?

"Here's one last thing Lito wanted you to have. It was his by right of being the leader of the group, but he could never sell it. Even when his family was hungry something within him kept him from selling it."

Quinn stared with amazement as the camera zoomed into the object lying in Lito's palm. His wedding ring. With trembling fingers he tore open the small white envelope. Onto the desk fell the simple gold band Cassie had placed on his finger that beautiful day when they'd become man and wife.

Here was his miracle, the one he'd asked the Lord for. He slipped the band onto his finger and stared at it. He'd lost weight since he'd last worn it so it was a little loose but it looked so right on his hand. It was back where it was supposed to be and Quinn needed to be back where he was supposed to be too, at the Lord's feet and Cassie's side.

Quinn slipped to his knees, grief and regret weighing heavily on him. He braced his hands on the floor and bowed his head. "Forgive me, Father. It was not You who failed me, but I who failed You. And Cassie. I have failed my family so miserably. You asked me to be faithful to You and yet I wasn't strong enough to maintain my faith in the midst of adversity. I doubted You and turned away when You were by my side. I ignored the opportunities to share Your gospel with my captors. My calling as a missionary was to share Your word with the world and yet I didn't see the mission field You gave me.

"Forgive me, Father. Please give me the peace and wisdom to make things right with my family. With Cassie. I pray she will see past my failures and accept me as her husband once again. And prepare my heart to be a missionary once again. That is what You have called me to be and that is what I long to be."

Quinn stayed bowed for a few moments and then sat back on his heels. He lifted a hand to his cheek and felt the dampness of his tears there. His spirit was broken but yet strangely whole. The stubbornness, the anger and the wall he'd built around his heart had broken away.

Weary, Quinn lifted his gaze to the laptop screen and saw only snow where there had once been a picture. He'd missed the last of the video. Moving slowly he sat back on the chair to restart the DVD. He wanted to watch again. This time with eyes not blinded by anger and hatred.

Tears flowed as he listened to the softly spoken Spanish words uttered by a man who had, at one time, held Quinn's very life in his hands. Quinn was thankful that God had been able to use him to reach at least one man before the anger and hatred had gripped his heart and soul.

Quinn wanted to watch the video again when it ended but it was already late and the days ahead were going to be emotional and he needed his rest. In the dark of his room, Quinn lay on his back, turning the ring on his finger and thanking God for giving him a second chance.

Chapter Fourteen

An unusually subdued Quinn came by the next morning. Cassie wondered if it had to do with the package or the prospect of the funeral that lay ahead. She wanted to ask but once again held her tongue. He'd tell her when, or if, he wanted her to know.

"Don't forget I have show and tell today, Mama," Jani reminded her as she finished off the last of her orange juice. "I want to take my daddy book."

"I don't know, Jani. I really don't want anything to happen to that." Cassie took the glass Jani held out to her, trying to ignore the pleading look on her daughter's face.

"Her daddy book?" Quinn asked.

Cassie looked over to where he sat at the table, his breakfast hardly touched. Something really was wrong. "It's a book we made together with pictures of you. It was for her to get to know you. She slept with it under her pillow from the day we made it."

"How come I've only heard about it now?" Quinn brought his dishes to the sink.

"I guess once she had the real thing she didn't need the book anymore."

Jani pulled on Cassie's hand. "So can I bring it, Mama?"

Cassie looked down at Jani. "I guess so. You be extra careful with it though, okay? Promise?"

"I promise," Jani said with a vigorous nod for good measure.

"Go get it and put it in your backpack. We need to go."

As Jani disappeared around the corner of the kitchen, Cassie glanced at Quinn. He stood near the counter, his hand braced on it. He stared down at the counter, obviously lost in thought. Cassie had never seen him this way before.

Tension radiated from him, so palpable there was no way Cassie could ignore it. "Something wrong?" she finally asked.

Quinn didn't seem to hear her at first but then lifted his head and stared at her, his gaze unreadable. Finally he said, "I'm fine. Great, in fact."

Cassie frowned. He didn't look fine and certainly not great. She wondered what had caused the change in him. Mandy's name popped into her mind, and Cassie felt her stomach clench.

"I'd like to have a few minutes to talk to you sometime over the next couple of days. Do you think we can do that?" Quinn asked.

Cassie nodded. She turned away from Quinn not wanting him to see the panic in her eyes. Was this it? The moment he finally asked for a divorce so he could be with Mandy? *No. No.* She couldn't let herself think along those lines. It was irrational and totally not supported by facts at all. Her mind told her that…but her heart was scared.

She blinked back tears as she kept her back to him, trying her best to appear busy with the dishes.

"I'm ready, Mama." Jani rejoined them in the kitchen.

Cassie took a deep breath and blinked a couple more times trying to clear the tears from her eyes before turning around. "Okay, let's go."

The ride to the school to drop off Jani and then to Cassie's office was fairly quiet. Each of them wrapped up in their thoughts. Cassie felt absolutely sick with worry about the conversation Quinn wanted to have.

As she put her purse in the desk drawer, Cassie wondered where her hope had gone. At one time she would have welcomed a conversation with Quinn but now… Now, the thought of talking with him about their relationship only produced a pit of dread in her stomach.

*****

The day passed quickly and soon Quinn and Jani were there to pick her up. She gathered her things and said goodbye to the staff before leaving the office. She wouldn't be back to work until the following Monday.

Quinn sat waiting in the car. He was leaning forward, his forearms resting on the wheel, staring out the front window. When she opened the door he turned to look at her. Cassie tried to read his expression but once again he gave no hint whatsoever of what he was feeling.

"We'll drop Jani off at the bookstore, right?" Quinn asked as he backed out of the parking spot.

"Yes. Renee said she'd take her by to get her things at the house later."

"Can't I come too?" Jani asked from her seat behind them.

Cassie turned to look at her daughter. "I'm sorry, sweetheart, this trip is just for Mama and Daddy. You'll stay with Auntie Renee for two nights and then we'll be back. We'll do something special on Saturday. You think of what you'd like to do, okay?"

Jani's little lip slid out a bit but she sucked it back in and nodded. "You mean like Nickelodeon Universe at the Mall of America?"

Cassie smiled. "Something like that."

"Okay, I'll think of something." Jani smiled and seemed to accept the deal Cassie had offered.

She danced ahead of them into the bookstore and headed right to the counter.

"Hi Renee, here's your charge," Quinn said as he followed Jani.

"My little helper." She bent and kissed the top of Jani's head. "We're going to have some fun while you're gone."

"Just remember she has school tomorrow and Friday," Cassie reminded her. "Don't party too late."

Jani and Renee exchanged looks and laughed.

"That doesn't make me feel any better, guys," Cassie said with a frown.

"Go!" Renee made shooing motions with her hands. "We'll be fine."

Cassie kissed Jani, gave Renee a hug and then left the bookstore with Quinn.

Quinn had brought his bag from Renee's so they just had to go by Cassie's to pick up hers. She changed out of her work clothes into a pair of slacks and a light blouse. The weather channel earlier had said the Florida was having beautiful weather even though Minneapolis was experiencing cool fall days. She'd packed mostly summer stuff for the quick trip.

They made it to the airport with two hours to spare before their flight left. The terminal was busy with Friday travelers but they managed to find a small table and Quinn went to get them something to snack on.

Cassie tried to focus on the moment and not think about what lay ahead. She just wasn't looking forward to the trip at all. When it had just been the funeral as the reason for the trip Cassie had actually been anticipating spending some time alone with Quinn but now that he wanted to have a talk, she wasn't as happy about their trip together.

"Well, it's pretty quiet without Jani here to entertain us," Quinn said with a smile.

Cassie nodded. "It's never a dull moment when she's around."

Quinn stretched out his legs, bumping hers in the process. Cassie waited for him to move his legs away from hers but he didn't. Instead he left them touching and looked at the people milling around them.

Her emotions were swirling, soaring high and then plunging. Cassie hated feeling so out of control. She moved her legs back, away from the close contact with Quinn. Maybe he could handle it, but she couldn't. It made her too vulnerable and took her too close to emotions she'd tried hard to ignore the past few weeks. Everything had been on a basically even keel the past little while but now it was upset again.

"Are you okay?" Quinn leaned forward.

Cassie met his gaze, hoping he couldn't read the confusion within her. "I'm fine. Not really looking forward to the trip, unfortunately."

"Me either. It's kind of hard to find enjoyment in something like this." Quinn lifted his soda and took a drink. "Are you looking forward to seeing Aaron and Cecily again?"

Cassie nodded. "They arrive a half hour before us so they're going to hang around and we'll share a car to the hotel. They're staying at the same hotel as us too."

"That certainly worked out well. I wonder how many others will be there."

Cassie shook her head. "I don't know. A lot, I would imagine."

They finished their snack and left the table so someone else could use it and walked through the airport waiting for their flight to be called.

Finally they were boarding. Cassie had decided to splurge and get first class tickets. She figured Quinn would be more comfortable there and instead of having three people sitting in a row it would just be the two of them.

Cassie leaned her head against the window and watched the ground disappear beneath them as the plane soared into the sky. She closed her eyes and rested her head against the back of her seat. She must have fallen asleep because when she opened her eyes next there was a snack sitting on the tray in front of her.

"Sleep well?" Quinn asked as she straightened in her seat.

"As well as one can on an airplane." Cassie lifted the snack bag. "Pretzels"

"The choice was peanuts or pretzels. I seem to remember you preferring pretzels"

"I would. Thanks."

By the time she finished the snack and her drink, it was nearly time to land in Miami. She braced for the landing and breathed a sigh of relief as the plane taxied towards the terminal.

Aaron and Cecily were waiting for them when they disembarked.

"It's so great to see you guys again." Cassie hugged them both and Quinn shook their hands. "Wish it were under better circumstances."

"Me too," Cecily said, a sad look on her face. "This was such a shock after Quinn's release. We had hoped for the best."

"How is Mary Alice?"

Aaron shook his head. "Not doing too well, but that's to be expected at first. She sounded stronger this morning when I spoke to her than she did yesterday. It will take a little time. A lot of time, probably."

They gathered all their bags and headed for the car Aaron had rented. Having been to Miami before, Aaron had no trouble finding the hotel.

"Reservation for MacIntyre," Cassie said as she leaned against the gleaming counter.

The clerk looked on the computer and then slid a card towards her. "Just fill that out, please."

Cassie took the offered pen and filled in the blanks on the card and slid it back to the clerk.

"And your credit card, please."

After fishing it out of her wallet, Cassie handed it over. Soon they had the keycard to their suite.

Because it had been a long day and the next promised to be even longer, the two couples said their goodnights, agreeing to meet in the morning to travel to the funeral.

Cassie led the way to their room and used the card to open the door. She froze in shock as she looked into the room and realized that it wasn't the 2 bedroom suite she had reserved but instead was a large room with a king-sized bed.

"Um, I'm afraid there's been a mistake," she said to Quinn. "I reserved a suite, not a single room."

"If there's a problem, Ma'am, you can let them know at the front desk."

"I will," Cassie said, watching as Quinn handed the guy who'd brought their bags up a tip.

After the man left, Quinn turned to Cassie. "Don't worry about it. We can make do with this."

Cassie was afraid she was going to burst into tears on the spot. Maybe he could make do but she couldn't. *God, why did you let this happen? I can't handle this right now.*

"I'm just going to go down and make sure they didn't give us the wrong room. And if they didn't, I want to make sure they only charged me for the regular room and not the suite."

Cassie escaped the room and headed for the elevator. What had changed with Quinn? A week ago he wouldn't have been willing to even consider sharing a room with her. Why was he now?

In the elevator, Cassie leaned her head against the wall, grateful she was alone. She teetered on the edge of tears. All the upheaval of the past few days whirled around her, threatening to take her down again. One minute she'd feel as if she was in control but then the next everything plunged into disarray.

Be still. I am God.

Cassie opened her eyes and stared at the closed doors of the elevator. She took a deep breath. *Be still...* Cassie longed for stillness, for peace to calm the troubled waters of her soul.

Know that I am God. Cassie closed her eyes again. She rubbed a hand over her eyes. *Father, I'm sorry for once again forgetting that You are in control of all of this. Thank you for the reminder.*

Cassie took another deep breath and blew it out. She felt a gradual release of tension. By the time the doors of the elevator slid open Cassie felt more in control and walked with steady steps to the front desk.

"Yes, Mrs. MacIntyre, we've been expecting you. Allan said there might be a problem with your room."

Cassie leaned against the counter. "Yes. I booked a suite of rooms, not a regular room."

The man looked at the computer screen. "I'm afraid the error is ours. I'll have Allan go with you and move you to your proper room." The clerk handed her a piece of paper. "Please accept this voucher for a free dinner for two as our way of apologizing for the inconvenience."

Cassie smiled at the man. "Thanks so much."

Allen approached the front desk and took the keycard from the clerk. "I'll give you a hand with your luggage, Mrs. MacIntyre."

Cassie followed him, her heart feeling much lighter than it had minutes before. She still didn't feel up to the talk Quinn wanted to have but at least she didn't feel as if she were sitting on the edge of an emotional abyss.

"They gave us the wrong room," Cassie told Quinn when they got back.

Quinn looked momentarily surprised. "Oh, okay. So we're moving to the suite?"

"Yep." Cassie walked towards the bags. "You haven't unpacked anything yet, have you?"

Quinn shook his head. "No, I figured I'd see what you found out."

"Good. Allan is going to help us to our new room two floors up."

Within ten minutes they were settled into their new suite. Allan left, this time refusing the tip Quinn offered.

Cassie slipped off her shoes and carried them along with her bag into one of the bedrooms. She took her clothes out of the garment bag and hung them in the closet.

"Cassie?"

She turned and saw Quinn in the doorway.

"Do you want something to eat? I'm a bit hungry, so I'm going to order something from room service."

Cassie shook her head. "I'm not hungry. I think I'm just going to take a shower and hit the sack. Tomorrow's going to be a long day."

Quinn hesitated and then nodded. "See you in the morning."

Forty-five minutes later, after a nice long, hot shower, Cassie crawled beneath the crisp sheets of the large bed. It had crossed her mind to call Jani but it was late already and Jani would probably be in bed. Maybe they'd try in the morning before they left for the funeral.

Cassie flicked off the light and lay there praying for strength for the next day. She didn't know what she was going to say to Mary Alice. What could she say when her husband had made it home safely and Kevin hadn't?

"Lord, please give me the words to offer comfort. I pray she'll be able to rest tonight and face tomorrow with your strength."

Cassie turned onto her stomach, tucking her arms under her pillow. Surprisingly, sleep was not long in coming.

*****

Quinn finished off the last of the club sandwich he'd ordered. He washed it down a glass of orange juice and then pushed the cart into the hallway. After coming back into the suite he stared at Cassie's closed doors. He had so hoped to have their conversation that night but for some reason she appeared to be avoiding it. It seemed odd to Quinn since she was the one usually pushing the communication between them.

Quinn looked at the television in the corner of the room and the DVD player that sat beneath it. He hoped to show Cassie the tape. He'd taken his ring off because he'd planned to talk to Cassie first.

He wanted her to put the ring back on his finger, where it belonged.

Tomorrow was going to be terribly hard. It was hard knowing it could have been his funeral people were planning to attend. It could have been Cassie mourning the loss of her husband, and Jani the loss of her father. Why the Lord had preserved his life, Quinn didn't know. What he did know was that the Lord had, for whatever reason, spared him and he needed to make the most of the time he had left.

Quinn turned off the lights and headed for his room. A strange restlessness filled him, a desire to get on with his life. He'd been in limbo too long. Thankfully the restlessness didn't keep the sleep from coming. That night he had the best sleep since being released.

*****

Quinn woke slowly the next morning and squinted at his watch. At first he thought it was two hours until they had to leave, but then remembered his watch was still set to Central time. Move a bit more quickly, Quinn rolled out of bed and stretched.

It didn't take him long to shower and change into the suit he planned to wear. He didn't put the jacket on, hoping Cassie would tell him he didn't have to wear it. It had been ages since he'd last worn a suit and it would be fine by him if it were just as long before he had to wear one again.

He tried four times to tie his tie before giving up. He'd have to ask Cassie to help him out. Leaving the tie slung around his neck, Quinn grabbed his suit coat and left the bedroom.

Cassie's door was still closed so Quinn went ahead and ordered an assortment of muffins, fruit and juice for their breakfast. He wasn't sure what Cassie wanted but hopefully she'd like something on the tray.

He had finished off a muffin and was drinking a glass of orange juice when Cassie's door opened and she stepped out. Quinn felt a tightening in his chest. She was so beautiful.

Like him, she wore subdued colors. The jacket she wore was short-sleeved, ending just above her elbow. Like her pants, it too was black but had white edging along the collar and the sleeves. It was a double-breasted style with white buttons and under it she wore what looked like a white silk top.

As she came near him he caught the subtlest scent of her perfume. Light and fragrant, it was a familiar scent that drew him back in time. The morning sun shining through the window turned her hair almost white gold. It lay across her shoulders in soft waves. Quinn remembered running his fingers through it. It had been like silken threads slipping through his fingers. His hands itched to touch it but he restrained himself.

"Ready to go?" he asked.

"I think so. I'd like to call Jani before we go." Cassie walked to the table and looked at the assortment of food there. "Is this breakfast?"

"Yes. Didn't know what to get so I ordered an assortment of things. Hopefully something there will strike your fancy."

Cassie picked up a muffin and sat down with her phone. She dialed, nibbling on the muffin while she waited for an answer on the other end.

"Want something to drink?" Quinn asked, setting his glass down on the table.

"Coffee would be nice."

Quinn walked to the small kitchenette and poured a cup for her. He heard her greet Renee on the phone and then speak to Jani. He went to stand beside her and when she finished her conversation with Jani, she handed him the phone and took the cup of coffee.

"Thanks," she said with a smile. She moved out of the chair so Quinn could sit down.

He didn't talk too long to Jani. Not much had happened in her world over night. He promised they'd call that night and then hung up.

"Can you help me with this?" Quinn tugged one end of the silk tie.

"Whoa, it's been a while, but I'll give it a try." Cassie drained the last of her cup and set it on the table.

She approached him with a wary look on her face. More than anything, Quinn wanted to draw her into his embrace, just to hold her close. It had been so long since he'd allowed himself to think of being close to someone.

Cassie took the edges of the tie and began to loop the ends over each other. "Rats." Cassie pulled them apart and started again. This time she must have gotten it right because she patted it and stepped back. "Looks pretty good for not having practiced in a while."

"Thanks. Do you think I need to wear the suit coat?" Quinn asked.

"I don't know," Cassie said with a frown. "Maybe I should phone Cecily and ask her if Aaron is wearing one."

"Would you?" Quinn grinned. "I thought only women checked out what other women were wearing."

"Hah, it's smart people that do it. Glad you're falling in line with the trend."

Cassie finished her muffin and washed it down with a glass of water before going to the phone. She called the front desk and asked to be connected to Cecily and Aaron's room.

"Cecile? It's Cassie. We're just wondering if Aaron is wearing a suit." Quinn poured himself another glass of orange juice as he listened to her side of the conversation. "I'll pass that on to Quinn. He'll be wearing one too."

Cassie laughed at something Cecily said. "We'll see you in a few minutes, right?"

"So I've got to wear the jacket, huh?" Quinn asked when she hung up the phone.

"Yep. Aaron is wearing a suit so you should too."

Quinn pulled the jacket on, grimacing as he did. "It hasn't been long enough since I've last had to wear one of these."

"Hopefully you won't have to wear one again anytime soon."

They left the suite a few minutes later. Aaron and Cecily arrived in the lobby just after they did.

"Morning, you two," Cassie said as they approached. Like she and Quinn, they were both dressed in subdued colors.

"Morning," Aaron said. "Ready to go?"

"As ready as we'll ever be," Cassie said ruefully.

Aaron nodded. "Yeah, this is not a day I'm looking forward to."

They walked out of the lobby and into the waiting rental car. Aaron expertly maneuvered the car away from the hotel and onto a main street. Quinn was glad Aaron was doing the driving since he didn't have a clue where they were going.

"Today may be hard on us but it's doubly hard on Michael."

"Yeah, it must be hard to have been released knowing that Kevin had been killed." Quinn was experiencing some feelings about it too in relation to his own release.

Aaron was silent for a moment. "There's actually more to it. This is not public knowledge and even Mary Alice doesn't know about it yet. I'm telling you because you are both so close to the situation."

"What's going on?" Quinn asked.

"We assumed after David's release that all of you had been split up for the duration of the captivity. What you told us upon your release seemed to support that. However, we've now found out that although Kevin and Michael were initially separated, they were held together for the last two years of their captivity."

"Really?" Cassie leaned forward from the back seat. "That must have been a relief for them. To have the support of each other."

"Probably," Aaron said. "But in the end, one of them had to die."

"What?" Quinn asked. "Why did one of them have to die?"

"From what Michael told us, the captors decided that they didn't want four deaths on their hands which is why you and David were released without incident. Unfortunately, they wanted the government to take them seriously and they figured that was being undermined by the releases. Killing one of the hostages was their way of proving how serious they were."

"Oh no," Cassie whispered.

"They flipped a coin."

Chapter Fifteen

Silence echoed through the car for several long moments.

"They flipped a coin to see which one they killed?" Quinn asked, his throat barely allowing the words to pass. "And Kevin lost?"

"Yeah," Aaron said roughly. "Kevin lost."

Quinn felt Cassie sink back into the seat next to him. Shock had robbed him of words. The breakfast he'd eaten that morning sat heavy in his stomach. Quinn rubbed a hand over his eyes.

"Does Mary Alice know about the coin flip?" Quinn asked.

"No," Aaron replied tensely. "We thought it best she not know. I'm only telling you now so that you know that Michael's situation is a bit different from yours. It's done a number on him, but he seems to be holding up okay."

The rest of the trip to the church was made in silence. Quinn wanted to reach out and pull Cassie close. He was so grateful God had spared his life but he felt just awful for Michael, living with the knowledge that his life had been spared because of a coin toss.

It strengthened Quinn's desire to take advantage of the second chance he'd been given. He would make things right with Cassie. He would continue with his counseling because he wanted to deal with his issues so they didn't encroach upon his future. And he would pursue the calling he'd felt years ago and follow the Lord's leading for his future.

A long line up of cars snaked along the street outside the church when they arrived.

"I'll drop you guys off, then find a parking spot," Aaron told them as he maneuvered the car up to the large front doors.

Quinn climbed out and went around to open the doors for Cassie and Cecily. There were television cameras lining the sidewalk. Quinn ushered the women past them and through the front doors of the church.

"Mr. MacIntyre?" A slender young man appeared at his side. "Yes?"

"Mary Alice asked that you and your wife, and Mr. and Mrs. Johnson come to the room where the family is. She'd like to see you before the service begins."

"We're just waiting for Aaron to park the car," Quinn told the man.

"That's fine. I'll be back in a moment to take you to the room."

By the time the young man returned a few minutes later, Aaron had joined them and Quinn had told him about Mary Alice's request. They followed the man to a room off the main sanctuary.

Mary Alice came to them as soon as they walked through the door. She hugged Quinn last and for the longest time. "I'm so glad you made it home okay."

"Mary Alice, I'm so sorry to hear about Kevin."

She gave him a watery smile. "God answered our prayer. Not in the way we'd hoped but Kevin is finally free."

Mary Alice's children came to stand next to her. They had been teenagers when their father had been kidnapped and were now grown; a couple had children of their own. Grandchildren Kevin had never gotten to see.

The door to the room opened again and this time Michael and his wife stepped through. Quinn saw a man who looked very much like he had when he'd first been released. Thin, to the point of being gaunt, darkly tanned with a shaved head.

Quinn and the others let Mary Alice approach them first, knowing she needed that connection with the last person who'd seen her husband alive.

Though there were some physical similarities between the way he'd looked after first being released and the way Michael looked, there were big differences in his attitude. He kept his wife, Susan, close to his side. They held hands and even when hugging Mary Alice didn't let go, giving her a one-arm hug instead. And Michael kept looking at Susan, as if not believing she really was standing by his side.

Michael and Susan's reunion had clearly been more successful than his and Cassie's. He just hoped it wasn't too late to rectify that situation between them.

Other relatives arrived, distracting Mary Alice and allowing Quinn to approach Michael.

He had no words as he embraced one of the two men who could truly say they understood what he'd gone through. Though knowing what he did now, Quinn couldn't imagine what Michael was feeling.

"Good to see you, Quinn," Michael said when their embrace ended. "I prayed daily that we would once again all be together. This wasn't how I imagined it."

"Me either. I'm not sure how to deal with this," Quinn admitted.

"With God's grace," Michael replied. "And with His strength. We'll get through it like we did the past six years. He brought us through it and took only one of us home. He must have plans for the three of us He left here on earth."

Quinn had so much he wanted to say to Michael, to tell him about what he'd gone through. It would be such a relief to talk to someone who really understood. Unfortunately, that would have to wait. They had a funeral to attend.

The pastor of the church came in and told them the service would be starting soon. The young man they'd met earlier came to them again and took them into the sanctuary. A section had been reserved for them, right behind the family pews.

The casket was closed but on top of it rested a large picture of Kevin. A younger version since the picture had been taken before he'd been captured.

Quinn glanced around behind them. The sanctuary was filled with people, there to pay tribute to a man who'd paid the ultimate price for serving his God.

Quinn felt Cassie press against his arm as she whispered to him, "Are you okay?"

He looked down into her soft blue eyes, saw the concern there and appreciated it. "I'm…I'm okay."

Her hand rested on his arm and he covered it with his own. Quinn felt her tense briefly but she didn't pull away. It was if she knew, even though they hadn't discussed their future yet, that at that moment, he needed her strength.

Quinn kept that physical connection with her throughout the service. When they stood to sing, he'd held her hand in his and had continued to hold it. Later they'd talk about their future but right then he just needed her beside him.

*****

It surprised Cassie to look at her watch and see that the funeral had lasted over two hours. The service had touched and moved her and many of those in attendance. There had been hymns, many of them noted as Kevin's favorites. Poems read by his children. His eldest son read the eulogy. Kevin's pastor gave a message of hope and redemption.

The most emotional moment was when Michael shared about their time together. Cassie found it hard to watch him struggle with his own emotions and there was not a dry eye in the sanctuary. Even from a distance Cassie could see how Michael trembled behind the podium.

"I want to share the verse that Kevin and I clung to through our years of captivity. It's found in Hebrews, chapter ten, verse twenty-three. It talks about us holding fast to the profession of our faith. About not wavering. Believing that God is faithful. Kevin did indeed hold fast to his faith and God was faithful. How I wish I could have been at Kevin's side to hear the Lord say to him, 'Well done, my good and faithful servant.' For indeed, Kevin was a good and faithful servant up to the very moment the Lord took him home.

"I was there with Kevin when his earthly journey ended. We sang together, not knowing for sure how that day was going to end for either of us. In the blink of an eye, he moved from this world to see the face of his Savior."

He bowed his head and cleared his throat. When he lifted his head, his eyes were closed and in the hush of the sanctuary, began to sing.

"Blessed assurance, Jesus is mine!"

As he moved through the first verse to the chorus, Cassie couldn't hold her tears. Then he began the second verse, his beautiful tenor voice cracking slightly.

"Perfect submission, perfect delight,
Visions of rapture now burst on my sight;
Angels, descending, bring from above
Echoes of mercy, whispers of love."

Tears slid down Michael's cheeks as he opened his eyes and lifted his hands as he sang the chorus again.

"This is my story, this is my song,
Praising my Savior all the day long;
This is my story, this is my song,
Praising my Savior all the day long."

Sniffles could be heard throughout the room as Michael ended the song. He didn't bother to wipe the tears from his face as he looked down at the picture on the casket.

"Though we are sad now, we will meet again with great rejoicing in the place where pain and tears have no hold. Thank you for your faithful example to me. I love you, Brother."

Shakily Michael made his way down the steps to where the casket was. He laid a hand on the top and bowed his head. Cassie couldn't contain the tears again as she watched Michael mourn his friend. How different his attitude was from Quinn's when he'd first arrived home.

Cassie glanced up at Quinn and saw a single wet trail along his cheek. Automatically she reached up and brushed it away with her fingertips. Quinn looked down at her and for the first time Cassie could recall since his arrival, his eyes were filled with emotion. The grief there was almost unbearable to look at. Cassie leaned her head against his arm and gripped his hand more tightly.

She and Quinn along with Aaron, Cecily, David, Michael and their wives were included in the brief service at the cemetery. It was only for the family and close friends.

Aaron parked the car in the lot at the cemetery and together they walked across the green grass to join Mary Alice at the graveside. Cassie clung to Quinn's arm knowing this would be the hardest part of the day. Nothing was as final as lowering someone into the earth.

Mary Alice wept softly as the pastor gave a brief message. She leaned on her oldest son, a single rose clutched in her hand.

Cassie's knees went weak. It could have been her. She could have been the one standing at an open grave, Jani by her side.

Without thinking, Cassie reached out for Quinn again. She slipped her arm around his waist and grabbed a handful of the fabric of his suit coat to steady herself. His arm came around her shoulders and pulled her against his side. Trying to keep the tears at bay, Cassie rested her head on his chest as she watched Mary Alice and each of her children drop their roses on the casket as it was lowered into the ground.

The pastor asked that the immediate family be left alone for a few minutes to say their final goodbyes. Cassie was grateful to be finally leaving the graveside. Quinn continued to offer her support as they walked back towards the cars with the others.

"If you are interested, I reserved a small room at a restaurant near here," David said as they stood in the warm Florida sunshine waiting for the family. "I thought it would be good for us to spend some time together. We might not get another chance since we'll be going our separate ways after today."

"I'd like that," Quinn said immediately, surprising Cassie with his apparent eagerness to meet with the men.

"Aaron, you and Cecily are welcome to join us as well. You've been a great support and friend to us all these years."

"We'd love to join you."

They waited to say goodbye to the family.

Mary Alice looked exhausted. "Thank you so much for coming. I wish we could spend more time with all of you but our family needs a little time alone together."

"We certainly understand," Aaron assured her. "Please don't hesitate to give us a call if you need anything."

Tears sprang to Mary Alice's eyes. "You've been such a good friend, Aaron. You too, Cecily. I can't ever thank you enough for all you've done."

She hugged Aaron and then Cecily but the hugs didn't stop there. Finally they'd all had a chance to say goodbye to Mary Alice. She waved as she turned to join her family near the long black limo they'd come in. Once they had left, the others got in their cars and went to the restaurant.

"I hope you don't mind, and please tell me if you do, but I'd really like it if the three of us men could spend some time together talking. The room is big enough we can sit at a different table." David turned to his wife. "Maybe you women would enjoy talking with each other too."

Cassie was glad that Quinn was going to have the opportunity to talk with these men. It would be good for them to share experiences and to talk with the only other people who truly understood what they'd gone through.

They ate their meals at different tables but then joined together for coffee and dessert. The conversation was light and at times humorous. Cassie's heart lifted when Quinn laughed at something Aaron said. He looked relaxed; the lines of tension around his eyes had eased.

Looking at him now gave Cassie hope that perhaps this whole experience would make him think twice about the decisions he had made. Maybe he would see that the Lord could truly work through tragedy and that He had a plan for Quinn's life. He had been spared. Cassie hoped he didn't waste his second chance.

Reluctantly the group separated as they left the restaurant. Michael and Susan were returning to California that evening. David and Emily were also leaving that evening but were going to Seattle. Aaron and Cecily, like Cassie and Quinn, were leaving the next afternoon.

Back at the hotel they went to their own rooms, eager for a chance to relax. Cassie slipped off her heels as soon as she walked into the suite, sinking her toes into the thick carpet. She took off her jacket to reveal the silk tank beneath and dropped down onto the couch. Rotating her ankles, Cassie watched Quinn peel off his jacket and draped it on a chair and tugged his tie loose.

His white shirt stretched across his shoulders as he reached to get a container of juice from the small fridge. He had filled out in the past couple of months but very little of it was fat. His regular physical work at her house and Renee's ensured he got plenty of exercise along with the larger amount of food he was eating.

Cassie allowed herself to think about how it had felt to be so close to Quinn earlier. She leaned her head back and closed her eyes. How she wished that closeness was the norm for them instead of the exception. Over the past six years she'd missed having someone to lean on, to offer her strength and comfort. She was so glad he hadn't turned her away when she had needed him.

"Cass?"

Cassie felt the couch beside her give. She opened her eyes and turned her head to see Quinn sitting on the other end of the couch. *The talk.* Tension flooded her. She sat up straight, all hope of relaxing gone.

"Can we talk?" Quinn asked, looking a bit wary.

Cassie wondered what he'd do if she said no but she didn't. Instead she nodded, not trusting her voice.

"I'll be right back." He got up and went to his room, reappearing a few moments later with a padded envelope in his hand. Cassie recognized it as the one that had come in the mail earlier that week.

"I'm not quite sure where to begin," Quinn said, shifting the envelope in his hands. "This week quite a few things came together for me. What I got in the envelope, talking to the men earlier and this funeral have helped me come to a big realization."

Cassie watched as he opened the envelope and pulled out a smaller one. Opening it he dumped something into his hand. He stared at it for a moment before stretching his hand toward her. Trembling, Cassie held out her hand and he placed it in her palm.

Puzzled, Cassie drew her hand back and stared at what lay there. A ring. More precisely, Quinn's ring. His wedding ring. Cassie couldn't believe her eyes. Carefully she picked it up and looked inside the band. Looked for the proof that it really was his. "Cassandra" was engraved on the inner part of the band. It was indeed Quinn's.

Cassie looked up at him. "How did you get this? I thought it was taken from you during your captivity."

Quinn nodded. "It was. When we were first taken hostage the guy in charge of the group that took me took it from me. I assumed he'd sold it."

"And he hadn't?" Cassie asked, still amazed at what she held in her hand.

"That's what this package was. He contacted a missionary and explained who he was. When the missionary realized what was happening, he set up his video camera to record this guy's story." Quinn settled back against the couch. "He said that he had planned to sell the ring. He needed the money for his family but he just couldn't. By the time he got to a place that would buy it from him he'd gotten to know me. In that first year I witnessed as much as I could to my captors. He was one that I spoke to the most.

"It wasn't until he returned to his home and thought more about what I'd told him that he began to search until he found a group of believers. There he found his answers and, remembering what I had told him, accepted Christ. Once he'd done that he knew he couldn't sell the ring. Instead he tried to find where the captors held me but it seemed that the rebel group suspected he would help me escape. Like I said, we'd spent a lot of time together. I think they thought he was too friendly with me. That was one of the reasons they replaced him.

"He finally heard the news of my release and knew I wouldn't be in the country anymore. That was when he started asking around for missionaries and finally found this missionary. He went to a lot of trouble but the missionary on this video said that he believed the Lord was leading his every step."

"I'm still having trouble believing it." Cassie looked down at the ring again. Her mind was in turmoil. What did this mean? Was Quinn just sharing this with her before he dropped the news of his plan for divorce? Or was there something else on his mind?

"I thought having it back would make you happy."

Cassie's fingers clenched the ring, the edges of it bit into her palm. She didn't want it back. She wanted to see it on Quinn's finger once again.

She held out her hand. Quinn leaned forward and caught the ring as she opened her fist. Softly she said, "I don't want the ring."

"What?" Quinn looked down at the ring and then back at her, puzzlement evident on his face. "I thought you'd be thrilled that the ring wasn't sold, that we got it back."

Cassie looked at him. Could he really think that a ring was more important to her than him? Did he think that she would be happy with a ring when their marriage was falling apart?

"I'm glad you got the ring back. I'm glad that man became a Christian. That your witness led someone to the Lord."

"Then I don't understand. You just said you didn't want the ring."

Cassie stood and went to the window, looking out at the city beyond.

She felt a hand on her shoulder but didn't turn to face Quinn. "Cassie, I don't understand."

"Neither do I, actually. Was this all you wanted to talk to me about?" Cassie continued to stare out the window.

"No, I wanted to talk to you about something else. Can you sit down so I can tell you about it?"

Cassie took a deep breath and returned to the couch. Here it comes, was all she could think.

"I talked at length with David today about his experience coming back to reality after captivity. It was unreal how much difference talking to someone who's been there makes. He understood things that I couldn't even put into words. He understood my anger. My confusion. My frustration. For the first time I was talking with someone who had been there."

Cassie felt like she was off-balance. Just when she thought she knew what was going to happen, Quinn threw another twist into the scenario.

"I can't thank him enough for what he's done. For listening but also for helping me see that I need to move forward. I need to put the past behind me and focus on the future. By focusing so much on the past I was sacrificing my future.

"I've also been going to a counselor, two of them in fact."

"You have?" Cassie asked, the news taking her totally by surprise. "When?"

"Usually during the day when you were at work."

"Why didn't you tell me?" Cassie was torn between surprise and hurt. Why had he felt it necessary to hide that from her?

Quinn shifted on the couch. "I wasn't sure it was going to make any difference. I didn't want to get anyone's hopes up if I couldn't make any progress with them."

"And did you?" Cassie asked. "Make progress?"

Quinn nodded. "I think so. I don't think I could have faced this trip and the funeral without the sessions I've had so far."

Cassie leaned back on the couch. She closed her eyes for a moment just trying to take in everything Quinn was telling her and trying to figure out where it was going.

"Are you okay, Cassie?" Quinn asked after she'd sat there for a few moments.

Cassie opened her eyes. "I'm okay. I'm happy for you, Quinn. That you've managed to work through stuff. I hope whatever future you choose brings you happiness."

Quinn stared at her for a moment, his gaze narrowed. "I must say this isn't quite the reaction I had anticipated from you."

"I'm not sure what sort of reaction I should have, Quinn." Cassie looked down at her hands. "I guess I really don't know what you're saying. I'm waiting to hear about Mandy."

"Mandy?" Quinn looked surprised. "How do you know about her?"

Cassie's stomach tightened. "I saw you having lunch with her at the deli one day and then you mentioned her in passing."

Quinn looked thoughtful for a moment. "Yes I guess we were in the deli together."

"I just don't want to prolong this any longer, Quinn. If you've decided that you want the divorce so you can be with her, just say so. Dragging this out is killing me." Cassie let out a puff of breath. Finally it was out in the open.

Quinn stared at her, eyes wide but suddenly they narrowed and Cassie could have sworn she saw a flash of anger in them. "What are you talking about? You think I'd be involved with another woman when we still haven't discussed where our relationship was going? You don't know me at all."

"That's certainly true," Cassie agreed. "I don't know the person you are now. At different times I've thought I did but then you'd say or do something that would make me realize that I really don't." Cassie rubbed her forehead. "I don't know what you would or wouldn't do. You came back home a different man. A man who'd lost his faith and apparently his love for me. What was I supposed to think?"

Quinn stood. "I need to get out of here. We'll finish this later."

Cassie covered her face as she heard the door of the suite close behind Quinn. The tears she'd been struggling to hold back finally flowed. Grief filled the corners of her heart; pain gripped every cell in her body. She shouldn't have let fear rule her! Even as the words had come out of her mouth she knew they were wrong.

Everything seemed to crystallize in her mind, turning her confusion to stark clarity. Quinn had not been planning a divorce. He'd been planning to talk about reuniting. As Cassie thought of all Quinn had told her and all she'd experienced with him over the past day she could clearly see he had been drawing closer, not pulling away. But she had blown it all by accusing him of something she knew, deep down she had really known, he would never do.

Fear and pain warred for upper hand within her. Fear that she'd lost Quinn for good and pain at that very thought. Surely he would give her another chance. At that point she didn't deserve one, but she hoped he would.

Please God, let him give me another chance.

There was a touch on her shoulder. "Cassie?"

The touch more than her name brought her out of her little world of pain. She looked up to see Quinn hunkered down in front of her.

"Quinn?" Her voice cracked. "Oh Quinn, I'm so sorry. I never should have thought what I did. I'm so sorry."

She searched his face for the anger she'd seen earlier, but it wasn't there. Instead she saw gentleness in his eyes and when he smiled it too was gentle.

"I'm sorry too, Cass." He reached for her hands and held them in his. "I reacted without looking at the bigger picture. You didn't know what was going on in my head, in my heart."

"But I should have known, I do know, that you would never behave like I assumed. You're too good a man for that, even the changed you."

"Let me explain, okay?" Quinn didn't release her hands, nor did he move from his position in front of her even though it must have been uncomfortable. "I know I said no to counseling before but I was beginning to feel like a boat with no oars or sails. I had no direction, no idea of what I wanted for the future. Then a couple of things happened with you and Jani that made me realize that I couldn't just brush off my family, no matter how I felt I had changed."

His thumbs rubbed the backs of her hands. "I didn't want to lose you, even though I thought you deserved better than what I could offer. I was not even close to being the man you'd married and at first I couldn't see that it didn't seem to matter to you, that you were willing to work on our marriage regardless. When I finally saw that for myself I knew I needed help, but I didn't tell you because I wanted to make sure it was something I could do. I didn't want you to get your hopes up that everything would be right between us only to find out I just couldn't work through things like I'd hoped."

Cassie had questions whirling around in her head but didn't know which one to put into words. Fortunately, Quinn didn't seem to want her questions just then.

"The woman you saw me with was Amanda Taylor. She and her husband Steve have been working with me." He smiled wryly and shook his head. "The funny thing about that day you saw us was that I was in the deli hoping to see you."

Cassie's eyes widened and her heart skipped a beat. "See me?"

Quinn nodded. "I knew that sometimes you went there for lunch. I went on a hunch that because it was Friday you might stop by. I just wanted to surprise you. I guess I did but not in the way I'd hoped. When I walked in I spotted Mandy there waiting for Steve. She called me over and I sat down to talk for a few minutes. I got distracted and must have missed you coming in and getting your order. I'm so sorry. Even if Mandy weren't married, she's nice but she isn't you."

"Oh Quinn," Cassie whispered through trembling lips. "So you're saying you want us to be a family? A real family?"

"That's exactly what I'm saying, if you'll forgive me for the foolishness I put you through when I first came home. I don't know that it will be easy because I'm still trying to deal with stuff but I'm hoping that with you standing by my side I'll be able to get through it."

"That's the only place I ever wanted to be, Quinn. I knew it wasn't going to be easy. Over the years you were held I went through counseling myself and talked with the wives of other men who'd been held hostage and released. I was prepared to do whatever was necessary to put our lives back together again. I'm just so glad we get that chance again."

Quinn drew her hands together and looked at her seriously. "I love you, Cassie. There were times when I thought I'd never be able to say those words to you again. Then foolishly I didn't take advantage of finally being able to hold you again and tell you that. How could I have ever doubted that I loved you still? You burrowed your way into my heart all those years ago and there's just no getting you out."

Tears streamed down Cassie's face. The panic and fear had long since fled replaced by a wondrous peace and overwhelming joy. "Oh Quinn, I love you too. A piece of me has been missing since that terrible morning. My heart hasn't been whole since you were taken, and I was so afraid it never would be again."

Quinn stood and pulled her up with him. He released her hands to capture her face and tilt it up. "My sunshine. I've missed you."

Slowly Quinn's head lowered and for the first time in six years Cassie felt the loving kiss of her husband. A sob escaped her lips, breaking the kiss. She buried her head in his shoulder, the sobs growing stronger. Quinn's arms wrapped tightly around her and pulled her close to him.

Cassie didn't know how long they had stood there when the sobs finally abated and she lifted her head. "I'm sorry, I didn't mean to cry like that. All of it just finally caught up with me. You're really home and our family is whole again. I'm so grateful."

This time she was the one who reached for him. As their lips she whispered, "I love you, Quinn. Forever."

*****

The water lapped gently against the rock. The moonlight created swirling pools of gold on the lake. Winter was coming and the wind that blew across the lake was biting but they were bundled up and didn't mind the cold.

Quinn sat with his arms wrapped around Cassie. Under them was a thick blanket and another one was wrapped around them with Cassie holding it tightly shut in front. Quinn felt emotions he'd long thought dead. It was like a major thawing had occurred over the past twenty-four hours. Everything had flooded his heart. And he'd come to a place of peace with God too.

Cassie had helped him see that through his witness a man had been saved. And in turn this man would hopefully share the gospel with others and the word of God would spread. At times it seemed a high price to pay for just one man's salvation but Quinn had come to realize that if God had been willing to give His son's life for him, he could give six years of his life for this one man.

He'd never have those six years back but what counted now was what he did with the years he had ahead of him. Right now he was concentrating on his marriage and getting to know his wife all over again.

They'd come up to the cabin the day they'd gotten back from Florida. Renee had gladly agreed to keep Jani until they came back to the city on Sunday night. It was important to spend this time alone with just the two of them.

Quinn leaned forward and buried his face in Cassie's neck, inhaling her special scent. He felt her pull the blanket tighter, her hands close to where his lay on her waist. Her fingers brushed his ring and stilled. Quinn felt her rub it and wondered if she was remembering how she slipped it back on his finger the night before. Or was she remembering when she'd put it on his finger for the first time. Both memories were equally memorable and special.

For Quinn the second time was even more important even though it had been done with only the two of them present and not the crowd of witnesses like the first time. To Quinn that time signified that they had already been through the worst and were still willing to go on together. And they would go on together.

They'd been sitting at the water's edge for thirty minutes but Quinn was ready to go in. "My blood's not as thick as it used to be," he explained to Cassie. "We can watch from the loft. From the bed."

Quinn heard her swift intake of breath and grinned. Cassie released the blanket and they stood on the rock and gathered up the blankets. Arm and arm they walked back to the cabin and to the beginning of their life together. For a second time.

Epilogue

Cassie stepped through the doorway and paused, looking around the room. Slight indentations in the carpet were the only evidence of the furniture that had once filled the room. Bare walls stood stark now that the pictures had been packed away. Where photos had once filled the mantel there was only empty space.

It should have made her sad, but it didn't.

Home is where the heart is. How true that saying was to Cassie and it offered her comfort. She was leaving the place she'd called home for her whole life. If the house could have talked it would have told of the happiness, the tears and the joy that had flowed through its rooms. Now it was time for someone else to fill the house with memories. Cassie hoped they would find as much happiness living there as she had.

"Are you okay, sweetheart?" An arm slipped around her shoulders.

Cassie looked up at Quinn and smiled. "I'm fine. Just saying goodbye to an old friend."

"Do you regret selling the house? We could have rented it." Quinn touched a finger to her cheek.

"No. We've committed the rest of our lives to the Lord, and I'm confident this is not where He means us to spend it. This is just a house. I will take the memories with me, in my heart."

A whimper from the baby in her arms immediately set her to swaying. She looked at the tiny face, cheeks chubby and pink with health. Baby Luke, the child she had prayed so many years for. God had finally answered that prayer and allowed her and Quinn to experience the joy of welcoming a new child into the world together. He was now just over six months old.

During the past two years they had spent much time in counseling, even more time in prayer and reveled in their renewed love. It was all Cassie had hoped for, and more. Quinn was truly free in all ways from the captors that had held him for those six years. He'd never forget that time, but it didn't hold him captive the way it once had. He'd finished his book and had it published. There had been a whirlwind book tour and now they were setting out on another journey, the next chapter of their lives.

In three hours she, Quinn, Jani and Luke would be boarding a plane that would take them around the world to Asia. What they hadn't packed into two crates to be shipped to their new home had been given away or sold. The only things that tied them to Minneapolis now were Renee and Esther. And while they would visit, it would probably never again be home.

Cassie's heart and thoughts were already focused on the new place she would be creating into a home for her family. She and Quinn would fill roles similar to those they had had in Colombia. God had brought them so far already, Cassie couldn't wait to see what He had in store for them in the future.

"Auntie's here," Jani, now eight years old, said as she joined them. "It's time to go."

Cassie handed Luke to Quinn and, with one last look around the room, she stepped out onto the porch and closed the door behind her. Carefully she locked it and then gave the key to Renee to pass onto the realtor.

While the goodbyes with friends and family were sad, Cassie held fast to the unfailing love of God, embracing the comfort it offered. She was secure in the knowledge that He would never leave them nor forsake them, no matter where in the world they went.

~*~ The End ~*~

Contact

Please visit Kimberly Rae Jordan on the web!

Website: www.kimberlyraejordan.com
Facebook: www.facebook.com/AuthorKimberlyRaeJordan
Twitter: twitter.com/Kimberly Jordan

Single Titles

Faith, Hope & Love

After several years in captivity, missionary Quinn is finally freed, but he returns to his wife a stranger. Will they be able to find their love again? Or will his lack of faith rob them of a future together?

Marrying Kate

She's loved him for years, so when he asks her to marry him for the sake of the children, she says yes. But will a man's determination to keep his secrets threaten Kate's dream of a marriage of love?

Waiting for Rachel

(Those Karlsson Boys: Book 1)

Though Rachel longs to accept Damian Karlsson's romantic advances, her secrets make her keep him at arm's length. But when her secrets are forced out in the open, will Rachel discover that forgiveness and trust are worth the risk when it leads to love?

Worth the Wait

(Those Karlsson Boys: Book 2)

Alex Karlsson is sure he's found the woman he's been waiting for. Serena, however, isn't so sure she fits the bill. Will long held ideals and secrets doom their relationship before it even starts? Or will they able to trust God when all hope seems lost?

Short Stories

A Little Bit of Love:
A Collection of Christian Romance Short Stories

Matchmaker, Matchmaker
Jani successfully found matches for other people.
Would she ever find hers?

From Jingle Bells to Wedding Bells
Not wanting to just settle, Deidre makes a drastic decision.
But is it the right one?

Sudden Impulse
Tannis was Miss Predictable.
Maybe shaking it up a bit would get his attention.

Fountain of Love
Three years later, Jennifer is back to ask forgiveness and get some closure.
Would long buried hope be satisfied?

Printed in Great Britain
by Amazon